Sanitarium Magazine
Issue no. 12

Thank you to all of our contributors, we couldn't have done it without you.

3

Contents

Thank you for picking up this issue and I hope you enjoy the stories we have lined up for you. Not to mention the great interview with Ania Ahlborn and we see where the horror happens with writer Kit Tinsley.

We are nearing our 1-year anniversary and as we do I feel I have to reflect on what we have achieved so far. Over 100 works

of fiction have been showcased. When we started Sanitarium we thought we would get a few submissions as we are a non-paying market, however the response has been amazing and I personally am truly humbled by that fact.

With that in mind we are moving forward towards our next milestone and we have a few surprises along the way - so stay tuned for those.

So, thank you again for supporting us and we hope you enjoy this issue. Who knows maybe you will become a subscriber or pick up a couple of our back issues.

Welcome to the Sanitarium.

Barry Skelhorn

Icy Waters

Philip Roberts

Physician: Dr. Roundtree
8245-AVD12

The shrieks and laughter of little children managed to travel farther than Jeremiah thought possible. With a street and the wall of his bedroom separating him from the jovial kids he had thought he would be safe.

Even on a normal morning he found these high-pitched noises to be particularly painful to wake up to. The three double whiskey sours, four or so shots of bourbon, and certainly no less than five beers from the night before managed to elevate his disturbance at the sounds of the laughter.

Even when cleaned up Jeremiah wasn't necessarily the most friendly looking man, and he could certainly imagine what people would think of his appearance now as he emerged from the bathroom, chin a mess of stubble, eyes squinting against the glare of the window he was approaching, and his clothes still stained with things he couldn't really remember from the night before.

The white snow magnified the glare of the sunlight, and just standing next to the window Jeremiah could feel the cold, but he found himself eyeing a group of kids near the far side of the playground. The group wasn't big, no more than four or five he figured, and all of them were staring at something on the ground. He might've ignored the whole thing completely had one of the children not walked into the ground.

It appeared as if there was a staircase leading down that a child had just descended, suddenly out of sight, while the others quickly departed, but not out of any fear, or so it seemed to Jeremiah. They walked slowly away from the spot, each going a different direction, until all of them were gone, and the vanishing child hadn't re-emerged.

Curiosity forced him to ascend to the second floor to get a better look at what had just happened. In the spot the children had been gathered all Jeremiah saw was what appeared to be a small, frozen over pond.

The answer hit hard. He didn't bother to put on a coat as he hurried down the stairs and out into the biting cold of the day. A chain link fenced surrounded the playground, wasn't easy to climb, but the rush of adrenaline got Jeremiah to his destination, chest heaving while he stared across the tranquil, undisturbed surface of the ice.

"But how did," he began, scratching his head, shifting around to look towards the school, towards the other houses nearby. He'd seen the child walk into the ground, which must've been this very pond, but there was no break in the ice where a child could've fallen through and gotten trapped.

The cold seeped into him. "You need sleep," he said, agreed, and started back for his house.

****

He left the memory of a vanishing child and an icy pond in the same mental trash heap reserved for drunken nights.

Jeremiah had found that most memories had a way of shifting in and out of focus lately. Near one in the morning that night as he sat in his second-floor game room surrounded by half-empty cans and bottles, he honestly had no memory anymore of a little kid walking into the ground.

In fact, when he moved to his window on a whim, the lights out in his own home, the only light to see by coming from a streetlight near the playground, Jeremiah simply smiled at the sight of what simply had to be a kid crawling up from out of the icy pond.

"How'd he get in there?" Jeremiah said to himself with a small smile, swaying while a child pulled himself upright, glanced around, and hurried across the empty playground. "He'll get sick."

****

Every so often memories had a way of digging themselves out of his mind and offering themselves to him, whether he wanted them or not. Two days passed before two separate memories connected and Jeremiah leaned forward in his recliner.

"You were drunk," he said, and he had been, but hallucinations had never been a symptom of his inebriation.

This time he made sure to put on his boots and heavy coat. Unlike before Jeremiah felt a pang of fear at the prospect of being seen when he lugged himself over the fence.

His flashlight lit up the surface of the small pond, the surface so smooth and clear, not a bit of snow covering it even though the ground surrounding it was coated.

9

The surface felt solid, like ice, he concluded. He walked home feeling foolish.

****

Work had been at a warehouse loading trucks. Those had been the sober years, after he had cleaned himself up. That had been the first job he'd ever lost without good cause, merely a victim in a corporate slowdown, one employee among a list of over two thousand laid off across the country.

Things might've been fine had he not heeded the advice of a friendly supervisor, unaware of Jeremiah's past struggles. "I know it's awful, but these things happen," the man had said. "Here, I'll tell you what. Take this twenty, go have a drink to calm yourself down, start-up unemployment if you have to, and you know, you'll get something soon. I'm sure of it."

Six months had slipped by in a haze, leaving Jeremiah in his living room, his head a mess of pain, while across the street he stared at the kids running out onto the playground.

Today he watched closely as the group of kids made their way towards the back corner of the playground. Three days of careful observation led to a notepad filled with little details. These included a description of the child just yesterday who had decided to take a dip in the frozen pond, only to emerge thirteen hours later when the sun had yielded to the night.

Once a child took their turn in the pond, they didn't appear to return to it, though he only had a few days of observation to prove this.

Just across the street the child descended into the pond. From the second floor of his home Jeremiah could see full well where the child went. They slipped below the surface of the ice as if it weren't even there. He saw only the faintest sign of a ripple before the child was gone, and the other kids were walking away.

An hour later, standing in line at the grocery store with a twenty-four pack in hand, Jeremiah couldn't help but glance around him at the other people and see those kids descending through the pond. How long had he lived in this suburb: four, five years at most? He couldn't shake the idea of a cult of some kind, of a town enthralled by something lurking in the depths of a small pond, captured when they were children, converted into something else. Were parents reporting children missing when they never returned home after school? Jeremiah hadn't seen any reports.

"That all?" a teenage girl asked at the counter, smile forced, but only in the kind of way Jeremiah would expect from a girl working a job she hated.

Never once in all those years had he seen an action that seemed out of place, a sense of wrongness of any kind. The store he walked out of was just as normal as any store he'd ever been to.

The worst of it all was the sense Jeremiah couldn't quite shake that none of it was even happening. Even before he'd been fired, he'd rarely made friends. Beyond the words needed to buy life's necessities, he hadn't spoken to another human being since the firing; his only company his own ramblings late at night.

****

Even a comfortable buzz couldn't quite warm Jeremiah as he sat near the bushes beside the fence to the playground. The time was never quite the same when the children emerged from the pond, and so Jeremiah had been forced to endure over an hour of waiting in the cold darkness, his last can of beer used up.

The crunch of snow alerted him to the movement. A hand rose from the supposedly firm surface of the ice and pressed down into the thick snow. The child was still dressed in his winter clothing from earlier in the day, no different at all, in fact, from the way he had looked when he first walked into the pond.
Everything about the act this child performed seemed nonchalant and commonplace. The only nervous tension Jeremiah could see in the child's actions appeared to be caused from how late the child was out, rather than the fact that he had just arisen from solid ice. Jeremiah's intent had been to grab the child, but his surprise kept him crouched down in the bushes until the kid was running off into
the darkness, and maybe that was for the best.

He approached the icy pond, rubbed the hard surface, and pulled out the hammer. The first strike sent a large crack through the ice. By the third swing Jeremiah's shoulder began to ache. In the low glow of the nearby streetlight Jeremiah watched the ice break apart, saw the widening hole begin to form, the whole thing so incredibly normal he just had to keep swinging, try to make it change.

He threw the hammer into the snow, dropped his hands into the opening in the ice, felt the freezing cold underneath it.

Jeremiah awoke, strewn over his sofa, eyes shifting rapidly across his living room. His first movement forced his eyes closed, his hands to his temple, mouth a desert seeking water. The journey to his sink took over five minutes, but a gulp of water managed to part the clouds.

After guzzling down a full glass he took the time to look across the living room at the remains of the night before.

The first surprise came in the form of a full bottle of Vodka. Wearing only boxers Jeremiah made his way to his living room table and the bottle waiting for him. He apparently hadn't touched much of it the night before: a pleasant little surprise.

The thing of it was he couldn't quite recall buying the Vodka. When given a choice he usually went for Bourbon if at all possible, not that he wasn't willing to branch out. So where had this come from, stationed so visibly on his living room table? Across the street he heard a child cry out.

Everything else came back to him. He was half dressed before he stopped again to stare at the Vodka, a bottle that suddenly contained an almost malevolent force.

Jeremiah marched across the street towards the pond and the three kids huddled close to it. "What the hell are you three doing?" he yelled to them.

All three immediately scattered. Anger let him scale the fence quickly. The pond had no cracks. But close to the edge Jeremiah knelt down and picked up his hammer.

"Who are you?"

Jeremiah turned towards the man walking up to him. "What's up with this pond?"

The man, clean cut and well dressed for the cold, stopped before Jeremiah, eyes scrutinizing him, judging what kind of threat Jeremiah might be. "You can't just enter here without a reason. I was told you were harassing some of my students."

"You know what your students have been doing? You seen them walk into this pond?"

The man glanced down at the smooth surface of the ice. "I'm not going to argue with you. I want you to leave right now or I'll have to call the cops."

"So, you do know, don't you? Must know. After all, a kid has to be missing from one of the classrooms every few days. Ever think to consider where the kid went? No, you already know where he went."

"I'm not in the mood to deal with this shit. Get off our property right now." He pulled out a cell phone as he spoke. "I'm watching, and I'm about to call the police."

For just a second Jeremiah almost took a swing at the man, wanting so desperately to get some answers, but what would it accomplish?

"Fine, but I've seen what's been going on."

He could feel the eyes watching him all the way until he stepped through his front door.

He dropped into his recliner, frowned at the dark TV, trying to get his mind straight, to figure out some kind of answer.

Something plucked at him that he didn't like. "Suppose this is some weird supernatural cult thing," he said to the bottle of Vodka. "Say all the adults around here went in that pond as a kid and now they're possessed. What about the people who didn't grow up here? Suburb ain't that small, and I know I'm not alone, so there has to be a lot of people who don't know about this at all."

Probably are, so what of it, his mind retorted. Doesn't mean they know anything about it, and that doesn't mean adults aren't being put through that pond. Hell, might be more than one of them, all across the suburb.

"Might be, but that isn't the problem." He bit his lower lip, right leg thumping repeatedly against the side of the chair. "Why is it so out in the open? Not like I'm in the only house that can see what they're doing, and those kids are going into that pond in broad daylight. Sure they come out at night, but anyone can see them go in. If this is such a bizarre secret, they're sure doing a piss poor job of hiding it if a guy like you can figure it out."

Maybe, his mind began, but he couldn't find an answer.

"But that isn't the worst of it. This binge you're on, you've never been on one this long before. Maybe you really are just making it all up, and that Vodka there isn't part of an evil plan, you just bought it and forgot. How much of your life is blacked out, so why is it so strange you'd forget you bought a bottle of Vodka?"

Suddenly it didn't seem very strange at all, and if the Vodka wasn't strange, he saw no reason why he shouldn't be allowed to drink it.

The first gulp eased back the headache and the twitch in his muscles.

After the second gulp he leaned forward. "Fact one: it makes no sense they'd be doing this in the open—count against it being real. Fact two: you found your hammer by the pond, so you were there, and if that memory is real, why wouldn't breaking the ice be real? Same with seeing a boy walk out of the water, but the ice is sure fixed up now. Doesn't feel right that this is just in my head. Too much doesn't add up."

It didn't make sense to him, and he needed some kind of answer before he could go forward. No adult was going to say anything, but a kid might be capable of being scared into spilling the truth, especially a kid who had just emerged from an icy pond.

****

He once again brought his hammer. Three days had passed since he confronted a teacher and took care of the Vodka. The nervous tension alone had been enough to force him to a level of consumption he'd never managed to achieve before. Even with the freezing air against his skin he still felt the sweat on his skin, the ache in his muscles.

No one watched the pond, no patrol meant to stop him from doing what anyone could tell he would eventually do. The thought came back to him right before the child emerged that if this was a secret cult, they were doing a horrible job of keeping it that way.

The boy couldn't be more than twelve, hidden beneath his thick winter clothing, dry even though he'd just emerged from what should've been water.

The boy had no chance to even turn before Jeremiah grabbed hold of his arm. He saw the child's pale face opening up in surprise when he turned to look at Jeremiah. The first scream the child uttered cut through the night, brought to life lights in the houses surrounding them.

A deep fury born more from fear than anything else raced through him in those first few seconds, waiting for the cars to rush up, for the voices to shout at him to stop.

He brought up the hammer by instinct; saw not a child but an unknown creature created from the pond. As the child pulled against his grip, shrieked again into the night, Jeremiah brought down the hammer towards the back of the child's head with all the force he could muster.

In his efforts to pull away the child's foot slipped out from under him, shifted his position, and the hammer struck the side of his shoulder rather than his head.

The child's struggles ended, replaced with a light whimper. Jeremiah felt his anger drain away. He looked around him at the calm winter night. He felt the bitter cold against his clammy flesh, saw the huddled form of the child still in his grip, and realized how close he had come to bludgeoning a human being to death. No part of him could deny what his intent had been.

He released his grip. "Get out of here," he whispered to the kid. The boy took only a few seconds to look up at Jeremiah, eyes filled with tears, before bolting across the snowy playground and into the darkness.

The walk back felt long, a journey that left his muscles sore, his mouth dry, flesh almost frozen over with icy sweat.

He had enough rational thought to understand how little the situation made sense. Standing upright in the garbage of his living room, lit only by a single lamp near the couch, he stared out the window at the playground, and asked himself why a child had just emerged from the pond. That was a question he couldn't answer, and he found it to be a question he didn't want an answer to anymore.

There were too many reasons he could come up with to doubt the truth of the past few days, and understood just as well he didn't want to doubt it, didn't want to believe he'd imagined it all, because to accept that would be to accept he'd nearly murdered a child.

The bottle of bourbon on the table in front of him was definitely his. The only truth Jeremiah accepted was that things couldn't continue on as they were.

He took up a seat on his sofa, the bourbon in hand, and stared at the empty screen of his TV. He started guzzling the warm liquid down. By morning he intended to drink everything left, absorb it all in a final plunge.

Perhaps he wouldn't even live through the night, he considered to himself, or perhaps he'd awake to find the past few weeks forgotten, thrown back into the trash heap of his mind, buried too deep to ever be found. He rather liked that idea.

Whether burdened with memory or not, tomorrow would be the first day he returned to his AA meetings.

If children were still descending into a frozen pond Jeremiah wouldn't know or care to know. He had his own problems to deal with, problems he knew and understood, and had bested before.

The only problem he cared to deal with in the middle of that cold, winter night was finding his next drink and forgetting about the past.

The End.

Case #39238

Philip Roberts

Philip lives in Nashua, New Hampshire and holds a Masters in Education and a Bachelors degree in Creative Writing. As a beginner in the publishing world, he's a member of both the Horror Writer's Association and the New England Horror Writer's Association, and has had numerous short stories published in a variety of publications, such as the Beneath the Surface anthology, Midnight Echo, and The Horrorzine.

A full anthology of Philip's short stories entitled Passing Through can be found on the Amazon kindle store. More information on his works can be found at www.philipmroberts.com.

Sweet Family

Shaun Adams

I awoke drooling into my pillow. Trying to remember what day it was. I had worked a week and had the next week off. I didn't have to get up today.

I lived in a Victorian semi, in leafy suburbia and drove haulage trucks through London to all points north. Today was the start of my week at home. I rolled over, opened my eyes, the red LED display on the bedside alarm read 6.30 am. My mouth was dry and my head throbbed.

"Can you hear that buzzing, I swear its coming from the wall sockets, it's making my fucking head hurt…honey?"

I turned to look at Jennifer curled up with her back to me, still asleep. Feeling peevish that she was not awake to listen to me complain I slipped on my boxers and headed to the bathroom.

I stood with one hand resting against the wall, the thumb of my other hand hooked into my boxers as I took that first long piss of the day. That's when I remembered the dream.

"I'll be seeing you, boss."

The voice of the hitchhiker echoed in my mind so stark I flinched, splashing the toilet seat. I had picked up the grey stranger on a southbound trip on a wet Friday night the week before.

We had talked to pass the time, he seemed eager to know about me, about my life. I dropped him at a Service station in the cold light of dawn, he waved, said, "I'll be seeing you, boss." Images of my cousin Victor came flooding back, replacing those of the grey stranger. Images of the way Victor looked back in '86, greasy tattered jeans, baseball cap back to front, shoulder length nicotine blonde hair. He was slouched against a graffiti covered wall, wearing a faded Metallica T shirt and a 'Don't give a shit' grin, he was my best friend, and he died in that year.

In the dream, Victor reached into the back pocket of his jeans and pulled out a cassette tape; he squatted down on the pavement. It's peppered with flat black splodges where people have dropped gum. As if by magic, his AIWA TPR 955 GHETTO BLASTER materialised. I watched as with exaggerated actions he placed the tape in the machine and pressed the play button. I hear the spaced-out tones of Jim Morrison. 'Riders on The Storm.'

Victor is dancing around the boom box, lip-synching, he points at me, the music sounds wrong, too fast. Screeching, hurting my head. The tape holder flies open spewing magnetic spools, squirming like muddy worms. I look up and see, not Victor, but the grey hitchhiker.

"I'll be seeing you, boss." He says. Grinning through teeth that resemble six-inch nails.

***

"Travis? TRAVIS!"
"Huh? Oh damn."
I woke up on the bathroom floor with my head jammed against the toilet bowl feeling disorientated and a little frightened. I sat up to see Jennifer standing in the doorway I was aware that Samantha and Toby were in the hallway trying to see past mummy. She was doing her best not to let our kids see me. I felt like Pinocchio getting his strings mixed up. The look on my wife's face hurt me, she wasn't just worried, she was embarrassed to see me like that.
"I'm... I'm real. I'm a real boy!"
The words were out of my mouth before I could stop them. The kids giggled but Jennifer's expression did not change.
"Babe, I'm gonna get the kids a drink, and put some cartoons on for them, then I think maybe we should make an appointment for you with Doctor Emery, Okay?"
I shrugged, pulled myself up, drifted back into the bedroom, and flopped back onto the bed.
"I think it's too late, Victor" I said staring up at the ceiling.
A large fat bluebottle described an erratic flight path across my field of vision landing on the opposite wall. Flies are my worst nightmare; according to Answers.com. Pteronarcophobia is the fear of flies. Well I had that all right, in spades. I grabbed a TV guide off the dresser and rolled it up. I slammed it hard on the wall, the crushed remains of the fly left an ugly black and red stain, I shuddered.
"I hope you're gonna clean that off the wallpaper?"
I turned; Jennifer had entered without me hearing her. She was carrying two mugs of coffee.
"Oh yeah, I will get some tissue, got the little fucker though. Flies, what use are they anyway, disgusting things."

I moved around the bed and took the Coffee mug that Jennifer offered; she motioned me to sit down on the edge of the bed. She followed suit. She reached out and placed the hand that wasn't holding a coffee mug on my knee, it felt warm.
"Are you going to tell me what's wrong, Travis, TRAVIS?"

***

I awoke drooling into my pillow. The buzzing sound, deafening. Something crawled over my face, vibrated against my lips. I rolled over, opened my eyes, the red LED display on the bedside alarm was barely visible beneath a heaving black mass of flies.

I turned to look at Jennifer curled up with her back to me, I knew she was not asleep. The smell was very bad.

I slipped on my boxers and headed to the bathroom; fat bodied flies bounced off my face as they circled the room. I remembered the children.

Cousin Victor stood on the landing barring my way. He looked so very unhappy.

"You don't want to see them, dude. Let it go. It's been a week now. You need to let it go."

I felt weak; I turned to look over my shoulder. Next to the rotting carcass of my wife I could see my own lifeless body staring up at the ceiling through sunken dead eyes, a fly infested tear gaped in the neck of my corpse. Black congealed blood stained the sheets.
"I'll be seeing you, boss."
I turned back to Cousin Victor.
"I guess you and me are both dinosaurs now, dude." He said.
"He killed us in our beds?" My voice sounded guttural.
Victor nodded.

I tried not to think about the grey stranger, being in my home, in my children's bedroom, I guess he's out there now walking the roads with his thumb in the air.

The End.

Case #63092

Shaun Adams

Shaun Adams lives and works on the Isle of Wight a small diamond shaped rock off the South coast of England. He has self-published two short story collections and been published by several online magazines and writing blogs.

Blog address: http://shaunadamswriting.blogspot.co.uk/

CLAYTON HILL SANITARIUM

Candy

Luke Tarzian

Physician: Dr. Edgar
9828-SJE41

Every Monday Mother takes her child to the candy shop on Main Street in the leaden town of Bumblegrub. Her eyes are always heavy from the constant lack of sleep, her ears afflicted with the incessant sloppy wailing of her chubby child. Just once, she pleads continually—is it possible just once for a peaceful night of sleep? But her cries are never heard, and so she rarely sleeps, kept awake for hours by the hungry crying of her fat and greedy child.

Mother walks her child down the trashy, graying sidewalk towards the candy shop on Main Street. The bulbous thing is waddling with glee, its mouth adorned with a sickly, chocolate circle, remnants from the treat that Mother fed it just to shut the noisy thing up for a moment. They arrive and Mother pulls the wooden door ajar, listening to the jangling of the bell. Her child scrambles in and runs around the counters in a joyous fit, unsure of what to cram into its sticky, frothing mouth. Mother stands just at the doorway, playing aimlessly with strands of graying hair. She's always stressed—it's been even worse since Father died: an aneurysm and a heart attack within a span of several minutes. Lucky bastard—free to sleep amongst the gilded skies in fields of cotton while she's stuck to labor on with no reprieve in sight. Just once...just once could she have a peaceful night of sleep?

Mother drifts into a memory and leaves reality for just a bit. She remembers how she used to cook and bake: her meat pies and her cookies were superb, and sometimes should would venture into candy making—chocolate-raspberry clusters were her favorite, and Father always said they were the best he'd ever tasted; Mortimer Beaumont, the man who owned the candy shop, agreed—and he'd been in the business of making tooth-decaying goods for decades.

Mother's pulled back to reality by the joyous gurgling of her fleshy child. Its face is rich with chocolate stains and syrup and its grubby fingers drip some sticky substance. Mother sighs and goes to pay the candy man, who smiles gratefully and thanks her once again for her continued business.

"I wouldn't mind a taste of those chocolate-raspberry clusters that you used to make," he ventures. "They were always so delightful—simply the best!"

Mother smiles tiredly but holds her tongue. She herds her dirty child out the door and walks the seven-minute journey home in silence, pleading yet again to her absent god for just one peaceful night of sleep.

Mother dreams that night of chocolate-raspberry clusters and a gilded field of cotton. In the center of the field is Father, waiting happily for her to join him. She's running towards him, quickly, anticipating his embrace and the taste of his lips. She misses him and wants to kiss him terribly. She's almost there, can feel his warmth and smell the sweetness of his breath. She's reaching out and—

Mother's sucked out of her dream, awoken by the violent wailing of her tubby child. Reluctantly she rises from her bed, stumbles to her bedroom door and heads into the kitchen to prepare an early morning meal she hopes will bring her some amount of silence.

After cooking, quieting the child, Mother crawls back into bed—but she wakes three hours later, drawn out of a dream once more, eyes embellished with the blackened circles of a bandit, as the yowling starts again. She's at wit's end, deprived of energy and strength, more fatigued than she has ever been. She's not sure how much longer she can do this; so she resolves to cook again. She sighs and rises from her bed, heading for the kitchen. Several hours pass and soon the dingy house is warm and smells like something sweet. Pots and pans sit on a lighted fire, boiling and burbling, melting this and that as mother sings. She's so engrossed in what she's doing that she can barely hear the gurgling and the wailing of her chubby child, doesn't pay it any notice.

Later in the day, Mother makes the seven-minute journey to the candy shop, carrying a neatly wrapped package underneath one arm. She pulls open the door, greeted by the jangling of the bell, and steps inside. She walks up to the counter, where the candy man is waiting, eying her with curiosity. She hands him the package, smiling tiredly, and tells him to enjoy. The candy man holds the package to his nose and breathes in deep, savoring the sweet scent of perfection. He eyes the raspberry liquid dripping from the corner of the package, pooling thickly on the counter. Odd, he thinks—syrup doesn't usually coagulate in such a manner.

Mother watches for a moment, then she bids old Mortimer Beaumont goodbye and steps out of the candy shop, listening to the jingling of the bell with weary satisfaction. She's free. Finally—she'll have a peaceful night of sleep.

The End.

Case #26807

Luke Tarzian

Luke was born in Bucharest, Romania in 1990 and has been writing since 2005. He's a graduate of the California State University of Fullerton, with a B.A. in English. He's an aspiring novelist, artist, a lover of cats, and likes to indulge in a nice Jack and Coke every now and then. He firmly believes that Grumpy Cat is his soul animal. He's influenced by a plethora of writers, most notably Edgar Allan Poe and H.P. Lovecraft, and is currently working on the second book in his *"Sewn From Seeds"* trilogy.

http://luketarzian.wordpress.com
http://facebook.com/rowesofficial
http://twitter.com/luke_tarzian

CLAYTON HILL SANITARIUM

CLAYTON HILL SANITARIUM

Close Cousins

Rob Bliss

Physician: Dr. Lotherton
6715-AED19

Norman Rockwell's painting, "At the Vets", with a small boy holding his bandaged dog in a crowded veterinarian waiting room, both dog and boy stared at prominently by a Great Dane which was being kept on a tight leash, hung as a calendar on the Executive Director's office wall. It was March 16, 1952.

The footsteps of the Executive Director, the head of the institution, Adamson, were mute rubber soles, but the heels of his newest employee, Doctor Gleemen, clicked hard on the tile. Adamson wanted to say something, but the list of accreditations, awards, revolutionary procedures, even several held patents of new surgical instruments and tools that were all a part of the new doctor's resume kept the Director quiet about a pair of shoes. Adamson could not lose Gleemen, he was too good, better than most, akin to having a Nobel Prize winning physician on staff: he made the institute look good and brought his expertise to bear on the medical techniques and protocols. Gleemen's choice of footwear was a mild irritant, which would surely be rectified once the good doctor began full time at the Newhaven Sanatorium, Batavia, New York.

Adamson took a pack of Camel cigarettes from the breast pocket of his white lab coat as he and Gleemen walked the pale green halls. He took a cigarette for himself and offered the pack to the new doctor. Gleemen smiled as he pinched a cigarette from out of the pack and leaned into Adamson's cupped hands where the lighter held a flame.

Gleemen exhaled up to the fluorescent lights and admired the glowing tip of the cigarette and the taste of smoke in his mouth. "I haven't had one of these since before the war ended."

Adamson squinted away the smoke rising from his nostrils. "I read your sheet, of course. Red Cross Ambulance Corps, along with all your other postings? Behind enemy lines, were you? That must have been interesting, to put it mildly."

Gleemen's gaze flicked up to see old threads from long dead spiders strung across the bars of wires caging a hallway light with a bulb, one of the older ones before they would soon all be replaced by fluorescents. *Caged lights*, he reflected. People smash the bulbs. You can eat a light bulb and not die, though it is a frequent method of a desperate suicide attempt. The glass of a light bulb is too thin to shred one's oesophagus or stomach. A doctor learns many things, and all of it becomes part of his intellectual kitbag.

"Actually, I was never behind enemy lines, although I did practice for both sides of the war … enemy wounded, of course, Hippocratic Oath."

Adamson held in his smoke, then spat it from the side of his mouth as he pointed his cigarette at the mouth of the doctor. "I couldn't help notice you have a bit of an accent."

"Swiss," Gleemen answered.

"Ah, that explains it. A good place to be during a war, I suppose."

Gleemen said nothing and continued to follow Adamson down the hall, into an elevator, up a few floors, down another hall. Gleemen was five-foot-seven, so his stride wasn't as long as that of six-foot Adamson; he walked quickly but always found himself a little behind the stride of the Director. Which was fine: Gleemen rushed for no one, but himself.

He finished his cigarette and put it out in a stand-up chrome ashtray lining the hallway. There were several of these ashtrays, so that a doctor or a patient did not have to go looking for one, and they didn't drop their cigarette butts on the floor, making the custodian's work more difficult.

The new doctor knew how to observe, which was the most important part of being a medical professional. His eyes always flicked from staff to patients, to a spot on the wall to a shadow to a man spitting a pill hidden under his tongue into his hand, then tucking it into his pocket. Men and women of various ages stood in gowns dotted with tiny flowers and stared through barred windows, watching the world beyond them. Sunshine and birds outside. Some of the people staring spoke beneath their breath, holding a dialogue between their present and their past, mumbling confessions and apologies and pleas no one would hear.

Sunlight formed geometric shapes on the floor tiles – a man in a wheelchair stared at them, calculated the diameter of each in his mind, then abruptly forgot all he knew of mathematics, of physics, of how to tie his shoes, of his name. This happened hourly.

A woman with lipstick smeared on her mouth stood at a window and used her short, painted nails to line up all the dead flies as a military battalion along the windowsill. A man sat at a chessboard, playing white, staring at the singe black pawn which had been mysteriously moved forward two spaces. He waited for his opponent to return. Most people watched television, or slept, or watched others sleeping or watching television.

A woman stopped a nurse to tell the good news: her son was coming to pick her up and take her to Siam. They own a cottage there. They were opium merchants. Her son was also her grandson. Such a handsome boy. Did the nurse know which way to the bus? There was a sale at Gimbels.

"In here are a few of our more severe cases, just to give you a feel for what we do, of what to expect. We hope your expertise can assist our endeavours."

"I'll try my best, of course."

Gleemen followed Adamson through a silent door on mute hinges into a small room. Four beds, three occupants, one of the beds having its sheets changed, the soiled sheets bundled into a cloth bag where it would be hauled to the basement laundry. The maid finished soon after the doctors entered, leaving them to their important discussions.

They approached a young girl with criss-crossed red scars like thick worms trailing up and down both arms. She was asleep, eyelids thin and blue, body limp beneath the thin bed sheet. Her arms rested at her sides, hands curved inward like seashells, and just as white. Her thin blonde hair had been combed by a nurse. The girl slept for sixteen out of every twenty-four hours. She wouldn't be waking while the doctors stood over her, but Adamson still kept his voice to a whisper.

"Shelley Barnes, 17 years old, multiple suicide attempts. Highly depressed, but also with a violent temper. She has had first fights with her parents and two younger siblings, managing to knock her mother unconscious on two separate occasions. Schools won't keep her, employment is impossible. We haven't made much progress on determining why she is so aggressive and depressed. We have her on sedatives, but when she is awake and lucid, she has been violent towards the staff. We've needed a straitjacket several times, moved her to isolation, remove rewards, the usual kind of thing. But we find sedatives keep her calm enough, so we hope to delve into her psyche during her calmer moments."

Gleemen nodded and lifted one of Shelley's arms, turning it slightly to left and right to see the extent of the scars. They were spidering bracelets around her wrists and forearms.

"May I?" Gleemen asked the Director, who nodded his agreement, though Adamson didn't know to what the new expert doctor was referring. Adamson kept a knuckle under his chin as he observed the analyses.

The girl's hand was kept aloft as the bed sheet was lightly drawn down the girl's body to below her knee. Gleemen bunched up the girl's gown to her upper thighs, to see what he expected to see. Deep purple scars snaked across both legs, above the knees, where a knife could do the most damage, and which would be easier for the girl to reach, either right- or left-handed. She was apparently ambidextrous. The scars were cross-hatched with fresher, thinner red cuts, with red halos tainting the skin along the cut line.

"We don't allow her to use a comb" Adamson commented, "or any other potentially lethal implements. Of course, lethality is a matter of interpretation, which we are learning to upgrade almost every day. Her teeth are brushed for her, her mouth held open by a steel mesh ring we have had designed – could be one of your patents actually, doctor." Adamson chuckled softly; Gleemen's dark eyes smiled back. "Her nails are clipped while she sleeps. We're not sure how she has made the fresher cuts," he said pointing in random circles over her thighs. "Possibly scraping on the metal frame of the bed. We once found that she had procured a paper clip, and had been hiding it in her vagina."

Gleemen pulled the gown back down the girl's legs, raised the bed sheet to cover her to her neck, rested her arm back over the sheet, alongside her ribcage. He looked to the sleeping eyelids of the girl for a few moments and nodded to Adamson.

In the next bed was a woman with the left side of her skull shaved, black stubble having grown back. A raised red and purple scar in the shape of a stretched letter C with pinprick holes on either side along its length took up most of the shaven part of the skull.

Eyes open, the woman stared at the ceiling at the caged light bulb, but she slowly moved her unblinking gaze to the doctors as they stepped to her bedside.

"This is Mrs. James, age 52, housewife and mother of three. She was admitted just two months ago by her husband. He had complaints that she was restless, sometimes depressed, but mostly argumentative and rebellious. He would return from work and there would be no dinner, the children would be eating whatever they could find in the cupboards, while Mrs. James had been in the bathtub for half the day. She refused to put on clothes, even when mowing the lawn. Why she was mowing the lawn was an oddity since that was her husband's job – attempting to usurp his power, possibly. The neighbours complained, police were called, but Mr. James was able to excuse his wife's behaviour as stemming from exhaustion and nerves. She told him that she didn't want to be a housewife anymore, nor a mother. She was a human being, not a slave. Told her husband and children that she hated them. Wanted a divorce, whether the church approved or not. Spent time in bars drinking, having drinks bought for her by strange men, going home with them, sometimes with women. Several Polaroid Land camera photographs were found in her purse showing her in, let's say, *delicate* positions with men, some of them Negroes. The last straw for Mr. James was when he came home early from work and saw Mrs. James having sexual intercourse with their German Shepherd."

Gleemen's eyes betrayed no shock, roving instead over the woman's face. She had no eyebrows; they had been drawn on with an eyebrow pencil. Her lips were chapped and her nostrils needed cleaning.

"Whose decision was the lobotomy?" he asked, chewing a tag of skin on his bottom lip, an action which pulled high his upper lip, exposing the noticeable gap between his large front teeth. Adamson noticed how boyish Gleemen's face was, could see the boy beneath the man, assumed he must be good with children.

"Mr. James gave permission after hearing our diagnosis, the sum of much work and speculation amongst myself and several on-staff and consulting doctors. We tried electroshock therapy, naturally, but some patients are unresponsive. She made two escape attempts, but our security personnel caught her in time – they once found her in her gown, unlaced and open, hitchhiking on the road that passes the sanatorium."

"And she has calmed since the operation?"

"She has," Adamson said, tucking hands into his lab coat pockets, gazing down at the woman. Her eyes had moved back to the ceiling. "Mrs. James," he called as though the patient were far away. "How are you feeling today?" Saliva slipped from the corner of her mouth as her eyes slowly moved back to the doctors. Adamson smiled. "You're looking well today. This is Doctor Gleemen. We're taking him on staff here – a welcome addition. He's an excellent physician who has had much success with hundreds of patients. I'm sure he'll help you feel as right as rain in the near future."

Mrs. James moved her lips without opening her mouth as though she were chewing on the smallest crumb of bread. Her mouth fell open, releasing more saliva.

Adamson patted her arm and looked up at Gleemen. "One more?"

They moved to the third bed where a young man lay, eyes open, breath inhaled deeply through wide nostrils. His stare stayed with the doctors as they approached, then focussed on Gleemen. Red-rimmed eyes that knew little sleep and thousands of nightmares. His skin was pale and shone with sweat, though it was cool in the room.

He swallowed thickly and his mouth opened and closed like that of a dying fish. The wet click of his tongue being sucked against his upper palate was the only sound coming from his white-dry lips. A thick strap pinned his arms and torso, and a second strap was tight across his upper thighs.

"Isaac Cohen, age 21, a holocaust survivor at Auschwitz. He was 12 years old when the Allied forces liberated the concentration camp. He had family in this country who brought him here, and subsequently sent him to us for treatment. He has very disturbing dreams and fits even during the day, thrashes his limbs, thus the straps. Don't want him inadvertently harming himself or the staff. He hasn't spoken a word since before his rescue, though there's nothing physically wrong with his vocal cords or tongue or lungs. Of course, the conclusion is that he was too traumatized by his experiences to return to normalcy." Adamson turned his eyes to Gleemen and hushed his tone by habit. "Plus his family informed us that he only speaks German. If he *could* make a sound, we would need an interpreter. Perhaps you are more of a boon than we thought. You speak German, I take it, being Swiss?"

"I do," Gleemen said, smiling down at the young man. Isaac Cohen's eyes expanded and his face quivered. An arm flexed and his bound hand tried to point a finger at Gleemen as the clicks of his tongue sped up. The patient's chest heaved and two fists hammered against the bed, his feet kicked. The straps held his body but his head and shoulders lurched forward. The doctors watched his tremors.

"Mr. Cohen," Adamson said sternly, putting a tight hand on the ball of bone that was the patient's shoulder, "please settle yourself." The doctor placed his other hand on the patient's other shoulder to force the youth back down against the pillow. "Please, Mr. Cohen, it's just a delusion, it's not real. Listen to my voice – concentrate on me – come back to reality."

The patient's eyes rolled back in their sockets as air sucked in to his lungs, nostrils flared and teeth clenched. With a blink, his glare snapped back to Gleemen.

Adamson glanced at the new doctor. "Could you get a nurse for me, tell her to bring a syringe, pentothal, usual dosage."

Gleemen nodded calmly and patted the chrome bar framing the edge of the bed. He leaned in and smiled at Mr. Cohen. "You were one of mine, weren't you?" he asked the patient in German.

Adamson craned his neck and looked over at the new doctor. "What did you say to him?"

"Just trying to reassure him that everything will be fine. Perhaps he just needs someone to speak his language."

Adamson sighed and nodded, pressing his full weight down onto the youth's thin frame, wanting to wipe a sleeve across his warming forehead but not wanting to stop pinning the patient to the bed.

"Well done, doctor," Adamson said as Gleemen began a slow tread from the room. "I knew you'd be a boon to this sanatorium."

Shortly after the new doctor left the room, not to return until the next day when his full-time duties began, a nurse entered with a syringe. Liquid squeezed from the needle into the patient's vein as Adamson held the arm still. The convulsions soon calmed.

The Director of the institution left the nurse with her patient as she watched over to ensure that the sedative took full effect, waiting for the patient to sleep off his waking nightmare.

With both doctors gone from the room, Mr. Cohen stared into the nurse's eyes and with a last ounce of strength motioned with his strapped hands that he wanted a pen and a piece of paper. Both were at his bedside at all times, growing dusty, in case he had ever wanted to write down what he couldn't, or wouldn't, speak. He had never used them before.

Isaac Cohen knew very little English, only what he had picked up quickly when the Allies appeared at the gates of Auschwitz and began processing the living and the dead, inspecting them all, trying to bring the half-dead back to life. American English, strange words and slang from New York and Texas and California and Michigan. He saw English words spelled next to German words on paperwork, saw that some words were similar in spelling and pronunciation, since the two languages were both Germanic in origin, linguistic close cousins.

The nurse put the pen in Mr. Cohen's hand and held the pad of paper beneath the pen nib. The patient couldn't see what his hand was doing from his restrained perspective, but his scrawl was legible enough for the nurse to discern two words.

"Gleemen" was written first, and below it was the word, or name, "Mengele".

The nurse looked at the spidering letters for a few moments as the patient's stare bore into her forehead, hoping the see a fearful revelation overcome her. But so few people could interpret, or even perceive, anagrams.

She smiled as she looked up at him and tore the paper off the pad, tucking it into the hip pocket of her uniform.

"Thank you, Mr. Cohen, it's very informative. Congratulations on breaking your silence."

She patted his forearm where he had a blue tattoo which would stay for the rest of his life. The patient's eyes slipped closed despite his attempt at raising them, and couldn't stay awake to see the nurse leave his bedside and slip quietly from the room.

She worked the remainder of her shift and took her uniform home. She did a full load of laundry, forgetting that there was something in one of the uniform pockets.

The End.

Case #38533

Rob Bliss

Rob has a degree in English and Writing from York University, Canada. His stories have appeared in multiple online magazines, including Pulp Metal Magazine, Twisted Dreams Magazine, 69 Flavours of Paranoia, Ideomancer, and Death Throes Webzine. He also has stories in two anthologies: "Bonded By Blood V" (SNM Magazine Press) and "Timeless Worlds" (Schlock Press).

Hate

Lathan Hayes

Physician: Dr. Lichten
6428-SED41

The boy sat in the small glen, the sun setting through the green tree tops above him. Cascading shafts of yellow golden light shot down through the branches illuminating the leaf covered ground of the small neighborhood woods.

He sobbed. The pain on his face was intense and burning, but a pain he was used to. He was a smart boy. He read every day; at school when he was bored with the work that was too easy, at home when his parents drank themselves into oblivion. He read to escape, for freedom.

The beating he had taken today were particularly violent. The other neighborhood children had started to understand that if they joined in with the bully, they might not become a target themselves. His beatings had taken on a vicious quality, the soles of shoes stomping down on him, their spit falling into his hair. Today he had been urinated on by a boy he had been in chess club with.

He held his knees closer; his shirt had been torn and now in the setting sun he felt the cold air of evening collecting around him. He shivered and sobbed again. He wondered what it might feel like to pull a blade across his wrists. He wondered if it would burn and then maybe he would just fall asleep.

A soft touch grazed across his bare foot; during the attack he had his shoes pulled off and thrown into the gutter. He opened his eyes and looked down. His eyes focused in the dimming light. A hand grazed across his skinned and bruised leg. A hand of shadow that seemed to be forming in the darkening cool air of the small woods. He should have leapt with fright; he should have run from the thing in the dark. He did not. The black hand of mist drifted up and touched his arm softly, taking on more form. He could see the shape of a man appearing before him sitting cross legged and reaching out touching him. He should have ran screaming into the night, but he had never been touched with such care before.

The shadow man sat in front of him, devoid of features, a dark image made of mist and shadow. The things hand reached up and caressed his face. He felt it press his chin upward, lifting his face. His bruised and bleeding nose pounded with pain. Blood ran down from the cut brow.

The thing seethed, and seemed to take on more form, a solid blackness in the now darkening world. The boy felt its hands on his shoulders. It bent forward and looked into his face. He saw no eyes, no face. Only a black reflective surface. His own bruised and battered face reflected in the dim starlight.

The shadow stood in front of the child and extended its hand to him. The boy stood and looked up at the man-sized thing. He took its hand and allowed himself to be lead from the woods. The boy could feel the thing drawing from him, like conjoined twins it shared his anger, his fear, his hurt and pain.

The pair stopped at the edge of the woods. It looked down at him, he could sense its question. He lifted his free hand and pointed. The darkness nodded. The boy began to walk, hand in hand with shadow man, leading it through the yards of the homes near the woods. The streetlights came on, as the deep blue of twilight gave way to the black and purple of true night. He led the thing behind homes. Dogs barked and then ran, cats hissed and fled beneath porches.

The boy stopped on a dark section of side walk in front of a rundown ranch home. Filth and garbage littered the lawn and a waste of a car sat in the drive. Light came out of the glass screen door as the boy could see the family of his torturer walking around in the house. The flickering light of a television reflected off the living room walls.

The shadow man looked at the boy. He looked back at it and then pointed his finger at the home. The thing let loose his hand and silently walked across the grass. Its dark outline seemed to swell with rage. It came to the glass door and passed through it as if it did not exist. The boy watched as his shadow friend disappeared into the home. A scream erupted from within. The sounds of struggle, of crashing furniture. Voices cried out in fear, in pain. The boy stared as a splash of red flew across the window. He could hear the bullies mother crying out again and again, and then she went silent as well. The ceiling light in the house swung back and forth playing light across the blood splattered picture window.

The shadow thing stepped through the front door and crossed the yard back to him again. It stood in front of the boy, strong and terrifying. The boy felt loved and safe in its presence. He took the thing by the hand again and looked at the shadow. It nodded at him. He started to walk to the next house, hand in hand with his hate.

The End

Case #86766

Lathan Hayes

Lathan Hayes is an emerging horror writer living and working in Dayton Ohio, USA. Lathan has regularly placed short stories for publication in anthologies and horror fiction magazines in the U.S. and U.K. markets. He divides his time between writing, working, family and stopping Eldritch Horrors from devouring the world as we know it.

Lathan enjoys fan contact and invites you to visit him on Facebook at http://www.facebook.com/LathanHayes.

CLAYTON HILL SANITARIUM

Bestselling Horror US

1 The Book of Paul - *Richard Long*

2 Under the Dome - *Stephen King*

3 The Remaining: Fractured - *D.J. Molles*

4 World War Z - *Max Brooks*

5 Sociopath - A Thriller (Jon Stanton Mysteries) - *Victor Methos*

6 Kill City Blues: A Sandman Slim Novel - *Richard Kadrey*

7 The Remaining - *D.J. Molles*

8 Doctor Sleep (Pre-Order) - *Stephen King*

9 11/22/63 - *Stephen King*

10 The Remaining: Aftermath - *D.J. Molles*

Compiled June 1st -June 30th 2013
Amazon.com Kindle Chart

Bestselling Horror UK

1 World War Z - *Max Brooks*

2 Bloodstone - *Nate Kenyon*

3 Chasing his mate (Lycan Romance) - *M L Briers*

4 Time Travel Megapack - *Various*

5 Don't Read After Dark: Keep the Lights On - *Carolyn McCray*

6 Shiver (Night Roamers) - *Kristen Middleton*

7 Sociopath - A Thriller (Jon Stanton Mysteries) - *Victor Methos*

8 Protecting his Mate (Lycan Romance) - *M L Briers*

9 The Mating Season (Lycan Romance) - *M L Briers*

10 The Remaining: Fractured - *D.J. Molles*

Compiled June 1st - June 30th 2013
Amazon.co.uk Kindle Chart

Group
Therapy
08.13
Survival Weekends with a twist.

Always be Prepared!
Words by Dombie Spens

    Zombie Survival Weekender (ZSW) is an exciting zombie
        themed survival training experience focused on team-
building, skill sharing and fun. We aim to engage customers on a
friendly, personal, level by both teaching participants and learning
from them. The main goal of ZSW is for every participant to go
away having learned something useful, having had a fun, thrilling
experience, to have met new people and built long lasting
relationships. ZSW is a unique mix of survival training and fully-
immersive, non-combat, live-action, horror-role-play. Zombie
Survival Weekender is the only event with so much depth and
content competitively priced with bespoke and corporate packages
available."

The Zombie Survival Weekender is here!

A mix of Survival training, Live-action Horror-Roleplay and a
party in a variety of exciting and beautiful places in South Wales.
isolated islands, creepy woodland, sand dunes, castles, mountains...

The weekender in Stages:

1- Arrival and welcome, safety briefing and going over the rules...
2-Team challenges, Survival Kits and Survival Skills share.
3-BBQ, Party, and Night live-action horror roleplay.
4-Games, Debate, Bragging, and Planning for the apocalypse.

Zombie Survival Weekender was the brainchild of me Dombie
Spens, it was summer 2011, I was daydreaming about zombies on
my island when I had an epiphany. As I stood on the foundations
of the old Iron Age fort on the top of my island being battered by
the wind, I imagined I was stood with the last of the survivors as
the Zombie hoard shuffled its way up the hill of the island
ominously toward us…

… I had to make this dream a reality, I first thought of writing
a story, then I thought of making it into a film, then I thought of

making it into a Roleplaying game, then finally I worked out I could make it into a full event…

Zombie Survival Weekender was born… It has been hard work, as lots of planning and organising goes into the events even in those beginning days. And the event is constantly evolving and developing to meet our customers' needs. So far I have made no money on the events but I have broken even in 2012. We have four events this year and are hoping to buy land and be able to run ZSW full time from 2014.

Our next event is ZSW VII: Pirates vs. Zombies on the 7th-8th September, tickets are still only £20 per person for the whole weekend! (Price will be going up next year) For full details check out the website: www.zombiesw.co.uk

All participants are required to do three pieces of homework; survival kit, skill share and costume (full details on the website), the more effort people put in the more they get out of the events.

If anyone has any questions about the events, the group or zombie survival please don't hesitate to contact Dombie Spens at: info@zombiesw.co.uk

or join the Facebook group which we use as a forum, or follow us on Twitter: @zombiesw

Soul Masque
By Terry Grimwood
Review by Casey Chaplin

Terry Grimwood has created a world with *Soul Masque*, where people have the ability to become infused with an essence called Glory, which when used properly, will destroy demons. However, this causes the Glory user to become ill, weak, and suffer in general, or at least that's how it is with one of the characters, the same character who is addicted to Morphine. Now, he's not meant to take his drug until after the job is done - that's one of the rules of the Church - The church being a group who regulates and delegates whatever job to its congregation. To me, this seems like Grimwood is taking liberties with organized religion, which I don't object to. I could be miles off base though, but if it's the case, it's definitely an interesting concept.

There's nothing wrong with the fiction per say, in fact the story isn't half bad. There are several connections between the characters in the book, and it's a good story of intertwining fates and consequences for not following the rules. It's interesting to see how the characters will do what they do. However, the length of the book dictates the flow and pacing of the story, which I feel is something that should never be done. A story needs to be exactly as long as it takes to tell - no longer and no shorter, and it seems that Grimwood wanted this piece to be a short work of fiction, and so he cut out some detail, causing the pacing to seem like a Formula 1 race. Sure, fast pacing can be a good aspect, if used in an exciting way. But in *Soul Masque* it feels rushed.

As I said, there is nothing wrong with the fiction, or the theme of the story. The writing is where I find issue. Sentences come off as too direct, or just not thought out. The pacing is poor, and the storytelling is just lacklustre. I didn't connect with any of the characters, and one could argue that is due to the length of the book, but I can argue and say that I've been able to connect with a character in the first paragraph of a book. The is a work that had high aspirations, but ultimately, I feel, fell short.

Every once in a while you come across a certain work of fiction, be it a movie, a book, a play... something that causes you to sit back and think for but a moment about what you just witnessed. Sometimes this is a good sensation, other times - well, not so much, and as much as I hate to say it, Terry Grimwood's *Soul Masque* is not one that brings thoughts of wonder and excitement. I feel it a duty of mine to be honest with my reviews, to let you know if something is worth the time and money to invest in. Unfortunately, that *Soul Masque* falls into the avoidance category.

VERDICT: 32%

About Casey Chaplin:

Casey Chaplin is a horror writer, reviewer, and content creator. He has written a full-length horror novel entitled Lizzy; competed several screenplays for production, and writes reviews for various websites and magazines including Gamers Mantra and Sanitarium Magazine. He has an education in Radio Broadcasting, with a major in Creative Writing and has worked both full time and freelance for several radio stations.

Classics Review:
Cabal
By Clive Barker
Review by Rob Salem

This month I went back and revisited an old classic, 'Cabal' by Clive Barker, and given the recent announcement of the impending release of 'Nightbreed: The Cabal Cut,' it seems rather well timed. 'Cabal' is a captivating and easy read, and an essential one for any fan of modern horror.

Any fan of horror is bound to be familiar with the film Nightbreed, which in spite of (or perhaps because of) poor box office showing when it was released has attained a cult status. Fans of horror literature are also as likely to be familiar with Barker's novella, 'Cabal,' on which the film was based. Published in 1988 along with several short stories from the final volume of his 'Books of Blood,' Cabal tells the tale of Aaron Boone and his encounters with and becoming one of the Nightbreed, a group of monstrous outcasts who call themselves the Tribes of the Moon.

Barker takes a different spin on the monster story with 'Cabal,' making the monstrous the heroic and tragic. He skillfully turns what at first seems like a typical slasher story into a brief but epic tale of biblical proportions and implications. While such a statement may seem like hyperbole and hero worship, the reality is that it is true. Looked at from the larger outside perspective, and considering subtleties in the story (and admittedly, including Barker's own comments on the film and its script), it becomes apparent that the story of Boone/Cabal is just an interlude in the much longer story of the Nightbreed, and one can imagine that the Tribes of the Moon are perhaps descendants of Cain, forever altered by the mark given him by God after the slaying of Abel. Further, the hints played at with Baphomet (supposedly the god of the Templars) and the infamous 'Burning Times' of the medieval witch hunts are sure and unsubtle hints that the story began long ago, and is far from being over.

Boone/Cabal becomes a sort of new messiah for the Nightbreed, coincidentally being both the destroyer of their world (Midian) and their intended savior, and is charged with finding them a new home in the wilderness of the world, much as Moses led the Hebrews from Egypt. Much like Moses, Cabal is initially reluctant, but Baphomet (who in Barker's description even echoes the burning bush from Exodus) reveals to him his purpose and gives him a new name.

Barker's impact on the horror genre at large hardly needs to be stated, and his mastery of words is obvious to any reader, and his relationship to and inspiration by the classic weird fiction and gothic horror writers is made plain by his style of storytelling. With 'Cabal,' he has successfully employed empathy to connect the reader with the monsters, making them the heroes we identify with and cheer for; each of us has some darkness in us, and reading Barker's work allows us to, even for just a brief moment, to embrace and enjoy that aspect of our beings without guilt or repercussion, and it is this that marks him firmly as one of the modern masters of horror.

About Rob Salem:

Rob Salem is a well-traveled poet and writer from Northern Indiana. He is lives in a quiet, rural neighborhood with his wife and son. He spends his weekends participating in historically oriented hobbies, playing guitar, and enjoying good cigars and good beer.

Look out for more reviews
on our website and
in our next issue.

COMPETITION

WINNER:
Jodie Watts

From the editors at Writer's Digest, this fantastic resource for horror writers details hundreds of magazine and book publishers who are interested in acquiring and publishing new frightful fiction. Each market listing provides information on where the publisher is located, what they're looking for, who to contact, how to reach them, and what their terms are. Each entry also comes with special insider tips for getting their attention. You want to get your horror fiction published? Start by looking here.

The name of the winner will be printed in next months issue.

Keep on writing and good luck!

The Cave at Black Hill

Kallirroe Agelopoulou

*G*o *farther.*

Just a little more...
There. Now you're good.
Now you can keep going forever.

A soft whoosh. How else to describe it? He falls softly, as if he never fell at all. Risky magician presenting another unbelievable trick, he does it on his own; he disappears from the face of the earth, but of course he didn't really disappear. I know he's with the others, in the same pile. Mass of bones and leaves. Rotten skin and fall wildflowers. It's a good place.

Something in me wants to see it again.

I move slowly toward the place I last saw him, his knees trembling. Toward the point where the dark setting of black basalt on the ground combines with the black mountains in the horizon, making you believe, when light fades, that you can continue walking forever. But you can't. Nature lies. The towering tree trunks that pop up from the depth of the schism, enhance the illusion. In the effort to reach across, before you know it, before you realize that you're actually trying to walk over chaos, you're dead. The edge is steep and the depth too big.

Every night, basalt and tree trunks. Black against black. An ideal natural trap is set, like a piece of some mad theatrical production. I lean carefully over the edge of the cliff. Everything is as beautiful as I remember, but I can't find my co-star. My gaze hunts the bright circle that my flashlight forms at the bottom of the ravine.

On the ground, among roots and pieces of flesh, something is moving.

A month ago.

I listen as they announce the course of action. They don't know it yet, but they are just setting themselves up for another failure. All their projects and ideas are always so very logical, but still... So far away from my reality. How could you ever rationalize the game?

You can't. You simply switch off your brain and play. My thoughts run along all of their hogwash. "Two-thirds of the region is a National Park."

Welcome to the real jungle.

"It will take weeks to scout the area with helicopters, months on foot."

No tree is cut, no bush is burned. They grow up and die in the same place for thousands of years, oblivious to people and cars and everything we've come to think of as 'the natural world'.

"That's why we should start quickly. We can't afford to have even more names on that list. They last saw them driving toward the south entrance... "

Thanks for playing,

"Let's start from there and we'll see what we can find." *game over.*

The Chief directs his voice toward the back of the hall, among the group of ordinary policemen who watch the proceedings, mouths gaping. "You! Send this fax directly to Washington. We're in the middle of nowhere, if we want to make any real progress, we'll need their immediate support."

I take the paper in my hands and answer with all the seriousness that I can muster.

"Right away sir."

***

Unexpectedly, the show goes on.

I saw him crawling toward the base of the cliff, with difficulty, but fast enough to disappear from my eyes within minutes. I don't run to open my bag, there is time. Wherever he goes, he can't get away. I grab the equipment, ropes, studs and rings. Ever since I started the games, I always carry them with me.

Descending, I make road between giant ivy plants and pointy dead branches, to the even greater mass of vegetation on the ground. I haven't seen this place for quite some time. Sun whitened bones, much less than I would expect, rest on abnormally soft soil, as if the whole earth fed from the disintegrated flesh. I'd like to lie down by their side for a while, but countless mosquitoes and the traces of blood that he left behind, don't allow me any rest.

When I started playing here, the cave at the base of Black Hill was a relief. The animals that most certainly hid in it, quickly cleaned the landscape from the great mass of corpses. There is no relief now, as I follow the broad, red spots, until they get lost amidst wild thyme and pine trees, deep within the dark hole forever yawning its gap.

Twenty days.

"Good evening."

The man on the podium is too young, with glasses and carefully combed hair that seems drowsed in gel. Obviously safe in his unpretentious, tidy appearance, he starts talking loudly.

"My name is Edward McCreery." He looks like a student of classical philosophical studies, like an old, nerdy friend that came to visit and not as the new head of investigations. "As you already know, we've recently stepped up our search for the murderer. There are a few things that I want to share with you."

However small, his opening segment was not even necessary. We all know who the 'exorcist' McCreery is. One of the most sought-after analysts in the country, an expert on ritual killings. Famous for his unorthodox methods in solving cases, like that one time he posed as a phantom in order to force a murder suspect to confess. With actual Voodoo ceremonies and made-up spiritual sessions going hand in hand with the traditional research methods in his repertoire, it's no wonder that he ended up with this moniker. The really strange thing is that someone thought *my* games would be a fit for someone with his expertise. It's still a mystery, the seed that blossomed this desire in me, but I can safely say that it wasn't a ghost that made me start playing.

"We didn't have much luck in finding any evidence of the bodies until now and this is our main problem in this case. The perpetrator's operating site is huge, even if we concentrate in the north, where most of the incidents have happened. It's a bit like we're looking for a needle between thousands of pine needles. If we were to separate the mess somewhat, I would suggest to do it geologically. And a little metaphysically, if I may. On one hand, in the northeast, we have the Beartooth, a nearly naked mountain range. Hard and rough, literally made of granite. We won't meet much life here."

He continues talking, with the entire room hanging from his lips.

And me among them.

"On the other side, in the northwest, the Absaroka. Different from all other mountains in the area. Sharp and pitch-black, with a large presence in the oral history of regional tribes. Thousands of years ago, the dark rocks were created when the whole mountain was a spectacular, dangerous volcano. Now it's brimming with life, plants, an almost virgin forest." He glances at the crowd for a moment and continues. "I think this is the area we're looking for. He hides them here, because this is the only place he can hide them in. Only here he can ensure the comfort of throwing them away without being noticed and without ever getting found. This is the spot that we must focus our efforts in, until we find at least one item that will further limit the field."

No one reacts. They just made their most significant step in order to catch me. And apparently the exorcist isn't even close to finishing yet.

"One more thing. What I have here, is an associative study of geographical and temporal parameters that deals with all the disappearances we've had in recent decades, not only in this State, but in the neighboring ones as well. It indicates that the case is much worse than we originally thought. Please, if I could have your attention for a little while more. First slide. The victim, Watkins, Mallory. Disappearance, the third of March, 1997..."

Mallory. For a moment I'm lost in thought, dozens of stray images mercillesly igniting my memory. My first victim, all blond hair and blue eyes and smiles, will finally enter the list. Without really finding her, they found her, recovered her from the anonymous pile of a hundred and more faces, no matter how well I hid her. I throw a small, irritated look, at the man standing on the podium. Awash in sweat, with an unimpressive physique, he has to stretch his hand to reach the screen.

But he knows how to play.

***

I slip softly inside the cave, like some miserably homesick snail. I'm prepared for the worst, which in this case is not so much my wounded opponent, but all the bears and jackals that might be hiding in the dark confines. At the slightest strange sound, the slightest movement, I have my gun ready to shoot and my legs ready to sprint.

The only thing I've come across so far is absolute deadness, from the moment I stepped my foot inside. It's impressive how much absence there is here, of any trace of life. No plants, no animals. I reach my hands around me. I don't feel anything, not even any familiar, incredibly soft

moss, climbing up the walls. Sea urchin that turned itself inside out, only hard, sharp edges spring out everywhere; up, down and all around. Stalagmites, don't they face downward only? And stalactites the opposite? Who knows what bizarre geophysical anomalies created all these stony knobs on each and every corner and surface?

I move carefully, in the center of the room, following the increasingly more sporadic blood stains on the ground. In front of me, as if blood spilled on the walls as well, continues a stone corridor with abundant, continuous red streaks. Jasper? Rubies? I ignore the embellishments in the rocks and I advance fearlessly into the passageway they form.

It swallows me to even greater depths.

Ten days.

They haven't found anything yet. The new head of investigations ceaselessly forms groups to patrol throughout the National Park, but the only thing that he has achieved so far, is to have a bunch of tired faces following yet another one of his meetings. The miracle cop hasn't even climbed to the podium yet and a middle-aged detective from the first row lifts a hand to ask him a question.

The first dismayed voice. Finally, the first reaction to this pseudo-individualistic, postmodern research approach.

"Maybe it's time to start looking elsewhere, away from the forest? Maybe in the nearby lakes? Even in this wilderness, after so many killings shouldn't we had found some dead bodies by now?"

Not if they're all in the same place.

"Not necessarily. I think that he has a favorite spot. In the woods. A place where he throws them, or hides them, if you'd like. I'm sure that it's not too far away from where he lives."

The answer, as if it came from my own lips. Who thought of it first, him or me?

"This is his favorite place in the whole world. He goes there whenever he can."

It called me my whole life. When I found it, the voices stopped.

"He goes there, because he wants to see them. We'll catch him, because he will continue to do so, even when he finds out we're looking for him there."

I turn my gaze toward the rest of the hall, annoyedly. They're all watching him with a mixture of admiration and disbelief. I lift my hand, more determined than ever. Time to tilt the scale. Time to put him in his place.

The voice that comes out of my mouth is creakier than I had hoped. "If I understand correctly, the right place is somewhere out there and we just have to find it? Even if it is as you say, it's impossible to scoop the entire region for traces. And if, somehow, we manage to do so, the nature of the ground here is such, that there will always be some piece of mountain that will elude us."

He doesn't seem deterred, his eyes twinkling with the anticipation of some hidden knowledge. I know the feeling. "This is what I wanted to share with you today." He keeps fumbling his notes aimlessly, with a half-smile. He is ready to share the secret with a formality, a matter-of-factness that he's sure to regret later, when he'll only have the faint remembrance of the revelation to hold him. He does it anyway. "With cautious optimism, I'm telling you that the scope of the investigations starts to narrow. We have our first items. This piece of cloth and a gold tooth, were found in the northern part of the Park by one of our groups. Today."

I watch silently, as part of my offering to the animals of the area is suddenly laid out in front of my eyes. I recognize the fabric. I've seen it before, part of an entire jacket, getting lost in a single, frightened move, along with its owner. I can't speak, my mouth is all dried up.

"Moments ago, we got confirmation that this is indeed a piece from the coat of Philip Launtier, the French tourist who disappeared a year ago in the region. I remind you that Philip, an experienced mountaineer, disappeared along with two more people, in an obviously *very* creative day for our murderer. His death was not an accident. "

The whole room suddenly fills with applause and shouts. "Where does he kill them? Tell us!"

He seems to be staring directly into my eyes as he prepares to indicate the point on the map. I

can't help but feel the deepest queasiness at the thought that he knows, he knows what nobody else can know. Only me. I watch with eyes wide open as his finger hovers dramatically, only to eventually land... Somewhere way off. Almost on the opposite side of the mountain, far away from Black Hill, from my hill. I can breathe again. Even if they check in a full twenty-mile perimeter from the point marked on the map, they still won't find me. Even if they could do that and I know that they can't.

I must think.

How did the pieces reach the place where they were found, if they were really found there? I can almost imagine wild animals ripping them with their teeth, carrying them like precious trophies, finally throwing them to the wind. Or maybe, as I suspect, it's all a lie, another one of McCreery's tricks to catch the murderer? It's a possibility, but no matter how I try, I can't read the truth behind the smile on his face. Who knows where the pieces were actually found?

With such noise reverberating in my mind, I clap loudly along with the rest of the room, among cheers and smiles, wearing the biggest one.

***

I'm going deeper and deeper inside the cave, my eyes peeled to the floor, ceaselessly looking for any crumbs of blood. Fresh air blows lightly into my face. The tunnels around me, continuing endlessly, forming intricacies and networks, they must end somewhere on the outside. There is sound here, too. A monotonous *bap, bap* dissipates into the atmosphere. Somewhere high up in another room, some rhythmic movement, like an underground river flowing over my head.

Each step and a sound. *Bap, bap*. And one more thing. After hundreds of barren yards, a trace of life. Somewhere in front of me emerges what looks like a terribly anxious tree, its branches thrown in all directions, desperate limbs forever trying to reach something. It can't be the sun, not in this place. They move, with small swings, as if gusts of wind are ripping through them. As I approach, I realize the illusion.

It's not a tree. From a rocky base on the ground and in place of branches, stone pipes pop up and then even more stone pipes, going up, getting lost somewhere inside the darkness of the roof. Moving, yes, with tense semi-circular moves, from one side to the other, like they're part of some giant cherubim's harpsichord. They shine, grey mixed with dark red, like the lines on the walls of the corridor I just crossed through. I approach one of them. What gives them their color, shimmers in the flicker of my flashlight, moving through them incessantly. I strike at the weakest hollow piece with the base of my hand and dark liquid gushes out. Upward and then, inevitably, all over my legs.

Bap. Bap, Bap. That giant, stone heart pounding louder over my head, I instinctively withdraw from the thick, red lake slowly forming.

One day.

Investigations are continuing unabated, however impossible they might seem. Everybody's on the trail of the found items, like hounds smelling prey, they'll not stop unless they find something. Three helicopters patrol and two infantry units have come to meticulously follow thousand-year old paths, all the way up, to the top of the mountain.

No one complains, they're working with serious eyes and steel convictions; all, so confident that my days are numbered. This is not surprising. Today's gathering, on the other hand, that feels...

Different. Just as it seemed that they were approaching me, that *he* was getting closer, something happened. A change. Invisible to the eyes and ears of others, but not to me.

Absaroka is not just a mountain, he says. Intimidating in the eyes of the people who lived in the area, sacrifices were made for the propitiation of the peak's influence on the human mind, for thousands of years. "At the end of each moon, only then were the animals offered. Only then did the gate open, the bridge between two worlds, a magical passage to some superior, divine field." He continues talking, looking at the crowd with urgency. "The murderer seems to be following these old legends and traditions. We are at the end of this lunar month, until the new one begins, we must remain vigilant." There's a great chance that the killer has Native American ancestry, he insists, with wild eyes. "He seems to reflect an atavistic penchant, a throwback to primordial traditions and customs, when the mountain range dominated the souls of men. Can you imagine what people must have felt beneath the amassing of rocks, in the shade of giant trees? All this wild vegetation in a pitch-black background, all the life springing up from the smoke. Dead, and yet livelier than the living! A product of godly welfare? What is the source of this ancient energy flow?"

He continues mixing his crazy theories with old stories, Native American tales of the area. The mountain, the voracious God. The sinkhole of the world. He reads to us from rare books, shows ancient sacrificial points on half-torn maps. But none of the people around me seem to mind. They don't laugh or yell, they don't react to the seer madness of his ideas. Maybe because they trust him, maybe because they don't know what atavism means, but most likely because they find a sense of relief at the idea that some 'outsider' is responsible for the whole situation. Not someone they know, not someone like me.

But I know the truth.

I should be glad for this shift in their research. Even if they do find my hill, they won't find *me*. And yet, all I think about in the midst of all this unexplained mental shift, of all this stupidity, is that I'm still in trouble. I got scared. I resisted the call. The bloody images of foggy mountains haven't left me yet, but they're not enough anymore. I've managed to avoid my playground for eight whole days, going back to the pictures inside my mind in order to feel again. I don't think I can stand it any longer.

That's why I'm hiding outside his house. I'm not thinking straight, but someone is to blame for everything and he's my clearest target. I watch him behind half-opened windows. He doesn't sleep either, sitting in the same chair, reading book after book. A bunch of maps and documents, for hours. Suddenly, he starts talking. For a moment I think he might be wearing an earpiece, but soon I realize what's going on. He's mumbling to himself, like a madman. Pieces of unfinished phrases unwittingly fall from half-closed lips, like his mind has to live a fight so big, it forces the words
to spill over.

"That which enters, must come out.
If this here is the end,
then, where lies eternal life?
That lives in death."

I silently watch as he continues reading and searching, more and more hysterically. My mouth is dry, my eyes hurt. He's crazier than me. I just want to play. Finally, he closes the book in front of him and lifts his head. His face alights, another hidden knowledge reflected in his features. I can almost hear the thoughts eating away at his mind.

I know I know I know I know

He enters the car with only a compass and a map and all of his rush, and I follow him, in the middle of the night, along the avenue toward the looming shadow in the west. Only the moon, a subtle, almost imperceptible slice above our heads, follows us. It doesn't take me long to figure out where he's going.

He's heading straight for my playground.

***

It's not that I didn't try to go back, back to the familiar haze of my hill, away from the darkness of this barren pit that seems to be gushing blood. I walked in from somewhere, I'm sure of it, but now the entrance is lost, missing, as if by magic. How did I lose my way? Did I get confused by the dark depths, the endless stone around me? I can only keep going, even deeper. The rhythmic beat, that unreal pounding of some hidden, perpetual motion, slowly disappears from my ears. Bones around me everywhere. I'm somewhere else.

The monster's lair is not pitch black, like all fairytales promised. Faint light from the edge of the room falls over countless osseous remains. It's enough to create here, deep underground, a blindingly white landscape. Half-digested and thrown into heaps, the darkness behind the piles, a possible hiding place for the nameless creature that brought them here in the first place. I walk among the bright hillocks and their shadows, carefully, with my finger on the trigger. If the man I'm looking for managed to pass through this place, then I can do it too. I'm heading toward the edge of the room, to where the light is. My only hope seems to be slowly fading.

I'm only half-way there when the opening is completely lost. The flashlight trembles in my hands, shimmering on the walls, searching everywhere for the exit. In vain. I'm swallowed in absolute darkness. No way forward, no way back, I'm trapped in this sunken ossuary, but not alone. There, behind the biggest mound of cracked bones, I find him at last. Between spots of dried blood, he's lying half-dead; coiled on the side, eyes closed, silently rocking himself. I reach to touch and he suddenly gets up and starts screaming, with a force that I could not imagine he still had inside of him.

"Thousands of mouths, stomachs, thousands. thousands of eyes, mouths, stomachs, thousands, thousand and all one!"

All of his energy seems to have gathered for one last blast, a last attempt to express with words, the storm brewing inside his head.

You don't know, he says. You don't understand.

"You're doing what they did."

No, I don't understand, or I don't want to understand. I just wanted to play.

Calmly seated again, he spreads his hands toward me, like a child ready to pat-a-cake. He touches me and starts talking, with a shrill voice that doesn't seem to be really coming out of his mouth.

"The last day of the moon. Do you feel it?"

My head is swarmed with the latest developments and all that they insanely, suggest. I don't realize it immediately, but something *is* changing around us. Bones begin to squeak, their small groans becoming more and more intense, as if something's pushing at them, harder and harder. I'm imagining a huge landslide on the surface, drifting through the trees and plants, a shocking disaster shaking up the mountain to its core. But something doesn't fit this scenario. The whole room seems to be shrinking, the white heaps forcibly reshape, joining together in a great buildup to the center of the room.

"It's getting ready."

Desperately, I touch the walls, I run along them, as they narrow more and more around me. I feel something, an elasticity under my fingertips. Uneven bumps that look abnormally soft, almost velvety, like suction cups. The room transforms, it's rebelling, it doesn't want to be a dead, rigid shell anymore. It's alive, moving, ready to crush us, ready...

"To eat us."

...and then dump us somewhere far away, maybe on the opposite side of the mountain, where the other digested pieces were found. Or even farther away, at another part of the world, wherever it is that its labyrinthine bowels will take us when the passage reopens. After it sucks from us all it can, leaving our bones to be twisted and squeezed at every meal, for hundreds of years, till they

crumble to dust. Thousands of eyes, mouths, thousands of stomachs. I know now. Moments before the end and he keeps laughing, but now I laugh along, we laugh together. So loud, that I almost miss his last words, whispered from within the darkness, the last thing on my mind before everything I remember is lost in one blinding flash of pain.

"They'll find it."

and then they'll know,

what they must do.

The End.

Case #74274

Kallirroe Agelopoulou

Kallirroe is a med intern with a severe case of scifi and horror addiction. Writing helps.

Some of her stories will soon appear in Villipede Publications' horror anthology, Darkness Ad Infinitum and in Dark Bits, a collection of horror flash fiction stories. Another one can be found online, in Issue 6 of Dark Edifice magazine.

It's been a while since she's updated her blog, kallirroe.blogspot.com, but she keeps trying to hit her daily writing quota, in Athens, Greece.

CLAYTON HILL SANITARIUM

CLAYTON HILL SANITARIUM
The Seeding
William Rasmussen
Physician: Dr. Peterson
S268-WCT29

Of course, Jason had been forced to plant the bulbs and seedlings himself, even though it had initially been Cassie's idea to start a garden, and she had actually gone out to get the little seed packets herself. But he had gotten used to it by now, the fact that she would invariably start something on her own only to rely on her husband to complete the task. He remembered just a few months ago when she had wanted the kitchen painted, and had even ventured out to buy the paint; her enthusiasm had waned then, and Jason had been the only one to pick up a brush and roller. Or late last year when she had decided to replace their worn living room carpet with hardwood flooring. They had gone together to Lumber Liquidators, where she had carefully picked out an inexpensive style, her interest piqued to the point where she had declined the store's offer to install it for a modest price, choosing instead to assist Jason in "their" do-it-yourself undertaking. Naturally, her role in the mission confined itself to handing him a tool or another piece of flooring, as if she were once again his supervisor.

But despite all of her faults, Jason loved Cassie deeply, still did after seven years of marriage…and three miscarriages. They were still young---he would turn thirty in a few months while Cassie was just twenty-eight---and had plenty of time yet to, hopefully, start a family. The doctor had advised the two of them that these things happened, but with patience and a little luck, they too would have a little one or two running around…the now-hardwood floored living room and freshly-painted kitchen.

As Jason stared out into their backyard that morning in early May, fully two weeks after he had first interred the various bulbs and twigs and seedlings in their smallish eight- by ten-foot garden, he couldn't help but be puzzled. Nothing seemed to be growing. There were no sprouts or shoots of any kind poking through

the moist, rich-smelling soil at all. He would have thought that something would be showing itself by now.

"Cassie!" he called. "Come out here and take a look at this." A moment later, his beautiful wife snuck over to his side. "What's wrong?" she said.

"This," he said, indicating the barren plot of earth at his feet. "Nothing's growing and I've been watering this thing every day now for over two weeks."

"It's too early," she said. "It takes a little while. I'm sure we did everything right."

"Hmph," he snorted, more at her use of the proverbial "we" than at his dismay over the growing process.

"Just give it a little more time," she said. "I'm sure you're going to love it when everything's blooming."

"We'll see," he mumbled, affectionately snagging an arm around her shoulder in spite of himself.

And despite her friendly demeanor, she almost imperceptibly flinched at his touch as if she had been shocked, coyly shrugging his arm off and withdrawing to the back door.

What the h--? he thought, shaking his head and watching her retreat. He'd noticed her icy disposition of late---couldn't miss it, actually, as it became more and more frequent in public before creeping into their bedroom---and wondered if her three miscarriages were at last taking their toll on her. And if, by association, she was now redirecting her disappointment, frustration and anger at him, in an attempt to clear her mind and absolve herself of guilt. Damn.

After the first two miscarriages, they had sought counseling as a couple, but more so for Cassie's benefit, since she was the one who had sunk like a drowning victim into the dark abyss of depression. It took several months, but eventually she pulled herself out of the murky depths and appeared to regain her once-energetic and carefree spirit. In a bizarre move, to Jason's way of thinking, she had then consulted with an elderly woman (suggested by a close friend of hers) knowledgeable in the ways of Wicca, a benevolent religious system based on a belief in gods, goddesses and harmony with nature. Jason hadn't understood her decision, much less the Wiccan religion, but after hearing out the benign, octogenarian Cassie had sought out, realized that if it helped his wife in some small fashion, he could at least be supportive.

What had bothered him about the whole undertaking was the fact that neither of them was very religious to begin with: he was a fallen away Catholic, while she was a one-time Baptist. For the two of them, time---both literally and figuratively---had conspired to pull them away from the weekly rituals of organized religion they had enjoyed---or, more accurately, endured---during their formative years. And for Cassie to reach out to some unknown woman, whose bonafides were questionable at best, in the hopes of using spells and magic in conjunction with nature to assist her in delivering a healthy baby after nine months smacked of pretense and ludicrousness.

But Cassie always got what she wanted, he reminded himself.

And that was all that mattered.

Except that employing these rather arcane methods still hadn't delivered the end result she had envisioned. Because after all of Cassie's "shenanigans" with the Wiccan lady, all of the "white magic" and "hocus-pocus," including visiting her for more than five months as often as if she were her very own mother, she had still miscarried a little more than nine weeks ago.

Needless to say, Cassie had been devastated, and had questioned the very significance of her life if she was deemed unable to conceive. But, once again, their doctor had nipped that line of negative thinking in the bud, advising her to relax for a while, regain her strength, be patient and let nature take its course.

And that was exactly what they were doing, Jason thought with a touch of doubt, before casting his gaze once again at their lifeless garden. He snickered softly, glanced at the warm sun and back at the empty patch of soil at his feet. Thus far, they had failed in their attempts to have a baby and, judging by their lack of progress in the garden, were apparently doomed to fail in that area as well. In a departure from his normally optimistic outlook, he wondered if they would ever be able to grow anything in their life.

Shoulders slumped in resignation, he traced his wife's footsteps to the back door and entered the kitchen.

"So…" he began tentatively in deference to the subtle tension physically smothering them like a shroud, "it's going to take a bit longer for our plants to grow, huh?"

"Yep. But they will grow, Jason," Cassie added with an air of finality.

"O...kay." He was suddenly at a loss for words, and filled a glass of water at the refrigerator for wont of something to do. "You never told me exactly what I---we---planted..."

She released an unladylike snort. "To be honest, I can't recall... I know there were some Sweet Williams...and some Pansies...but, other than that, I guess we'll just have to wait and see."

"Hmph," he said, gulping down the refreshing cold water, unwittingly exacerbating the already chilly situation. "Where did you get the idea about starting a garden?"

"Mrs. Magruder. I told you that."

Jason frowned, realizing that not only had the Wiccan lady steered them wrong with Cassie's pregnancy, but she was still meddling with their lives. "Is this something you really want to do?"

"Why not? She's just trying to help. She thought it would take my mind off of...my failure. You do realize she believes that communing with nature can only enrich and reward your life."

"If you say so," he mumbled. He carefully placed his empty glass on the counter and gazed longingly at his wife. She was a beautiful woman with long blonde hair and light blue eyes, who stood a shade over five-seven and favored Gwyneth Paltrow in the looks department, especially with her slight, curvaceous figure. "Are you mad at me about something?" he finally spat.

Cassie cocked her head and squinted at him from her seat at the table, as if thinking he was joking. "No," she said, shaking her head. "Why do you think that?"

"Well, it's been kind of obvious lately. The way you turn a cold shoulder to me, give me those pained responses, and the way you've been ignoring me in bed. I mean—what am I supposed to think?"

She sighed, stood up and walked over to him, her right-hand entwining with his. "It's not you," she said, staring into his face. "I'm sorry if you feel that way. It's just that...losing the baby is hitting me hard again. I've been feeling down...and I guess I've been taking it out on you. Shit."

"It's okay, honey," he said, running his free hand through her soft hair. "Just don't shut me out again, okay?"

"Okay, I promise."

Cassie stretched up on her tiptoes, smiled, and planted a sloppy, wet kiss on his lips.

A week later, when Jason stepped outside midmorning to inspect their thus far empty garden, he discovered to his surprise several tiny, green sprouts breaking through the soil's skin like hair follicles. He gazed proudly at the budding seeds, actually bent over a couple of them to gently touch the shoots as if to confirm their presence. Standing tall again, he examined the entire garden, and noticed that while a large portion of the area was sprinkled with the little, one- to two-inch sprigs, there was still a small section in the far-right quadrant that was bare.

Hmm, he thought. Wonder what I---we---planted there? He furrowed his brow in concentration before realizing that if Cassie could hardly remember, then he had no idea at all. Must be late bloomers, though.

Tearing his attention from the suddenly burgeoning garden, he made his way back into the house to let his wife in on the good news.

Despite his brief, warm chat with Cassie a week earlier, their relationship had remained fairly static. He still believed something was bothering her, and notwithstanding her recent denial, everything pointed directly at him and not her claim that she was once again troubled over her recent miscarriage. She had continued to keep her distance from him, as if they weren't married and were merely sharing lodging, and she had not been interested in making love in weeks, when before they had rarely let a couple days pass without jumping each other's bones. He was clearly at a loss to explain her unusual behavior.

"Guess what?" he said once he found her in the kitchen, making another pot of coffee.

"What?" she snapped.

Jason cringed inside at her sharp tone. "The garden's finally growing!"

"Hmph," she said, obviously unimpressed. "I told you to be patient."

"C'mon. Let me show you."

"Not now, Jason. Later. I'm in the middle of something." Stunned by her response and lack of interest in her project, he felt like a child who had just been disciplined.

"I was wondering..." she began, scrutinizing their dated kitchen Formica, "you think we should tear out this counter and install granite tile?"

Oh, geez, he thought. Here we go again with another renovation that I'll have to finish.

"I don't know, hon. Lemme think about it..."

Late that evening, while they were watching the nightly news on TV, Jason began scratching more and more frequently at his arms and the front of his legs.

"What's wrong, Jason?" Cassie asked.

"I don't know," he said, face grimacing, flushing. "All of a sudden my arms and legs are itching, kind of burning, and it won't go away."

"Maybe you ate something or touched something you're allergic to."

"Hmm," he said, unconsciously worrying at his forearms. "You know...I did touch several of those sprouts in the garden this morning. I wonder if that might be causing it..."

"Why don't you go take some Benadryl? It should stop the itching."

"Yeah," he said, standing up and heading for the kitchen. "Let me grab some now before I start drawing blood." He manufactured a half-smile for Cassie's sake, but she merely regarded him with the stoicism of a statue.

Geez, he thought once he was in the kitchen and rummaging through the medicine cabinet. Show some sympathy, would you? After he had found the right bottle and downed a capsule with a glass of cold water, he returned to the living room and told his wife it was late and he was headed for bed.

"You know how these allergy medicines tire me out. I might as well go to sleep. You comin' in soon?"

"Yeah, you go on ahead. I'll be there in a few minutes."

With a somber glance at his wife, Jason retired to their bedroom. As he lay beneath the covers, thinking about the events of the past week or so, a horrible thought struck him like a sledgehammer: What if Cassie had found out about his brief fling midway through her third pregnancy? Jeezus! he thought. It would explain everything! Her curt, snappy responses to him; her depressed mood; her coldness around him (especially in the bedroom) --- in short, her sea change toward their life as a whole. Shit!

But there was no way she could have found out, he was certain. She had been maybe two months along in her pregnancy, and she had been so conservative and cautious about everything: following Mrs. Magruder's instructions as if they were gospel, eating all the proper foods and taking the right vitamins...and cutting him off sexually. "For the sake of the baby," she had informed him. "You understand, don't you, honey?" she had pleaded.

He had bought into it for a while---after all, he truly did want to become a father---but when young, beautiful Elena from his office commiserated with him one day after work, one thing led to another, and the drinks lowered his inhibitions and her panties, and he found himself in bed with her. That evening and once more the following week, before he realized the error of his ways, and called a halt to it.

Elena wouldn't have told a soul; he was positive about that. Besides, knowing his wife the way he did, it wouldn't be like her to hold in her anger if she had learned of his unfaithfulness; for sure she would have had it out with him by now. Physically as well as verbally. So, what the hell was going on with her? he wondered.

And as he pondered the various possible scenarios that might explain his wife's unusual behavior of late, making a mental note to talk to Elena on Monday, the Benadryl kicked in and sleep swiftly overwhelmed him.

***

The next morning, a Sunday, Jason slept in late, a byproduct of the allergy medicine he had taken the night before. When he finally woke up, he found himself alone in bed.

"Cassie! Cassie, where are you?"

When his wife didn't respond, he glanced at the alarm clock---noticing it was almost 9:30---and tried to get out of bed, only to discover that his entire body ached and his limbs throbbed as if he had been run through a meat grinder. What the hell? The itching on his arms and legs appeared to have subsided, only to be replaced by an all-consuming soreness from head to toe. Geez, I must be coming down with the flu or something. Struggling to gain his feet, he slid into his bedroom slippers and trudged downstairs in search of his wife.

A quick canvass of the house failed to reveal her whereabouts, until he stepped gingerly out of the kitchen to their backyard and located her at the garden, peering intently at the myriad green shoots and sprouts littering the plot of soil and reaching for the sun.

"I was wondering where you were," he said.

She turned to face him, nursing a mug of coffee in her hands. "I was just checking our garden." She returned her gaze to the scores of plants, some stretching their legs seven or eight inches high.

"Jeezus, they've grown fast!" he said, mesmerized by the plants' progress and, for the moment, forgetting about his overriding discomfort. The rectangular patch of earth was now blanketed by short green stalks---some thin, some fat, some with multiple shoots; all of them growing at a remarkable pace---except for the far-right corner, whose small square of soil was still devoid of any sign of plant life.

"I wonder why nothing's growing over there," he said, indicating the bare earth in the corner when she looked his way.

"Hmm...I have no idea," she said. She sipped at her coffee. Realizing his attempts at warm conversation were once again being met by a cold shoulder, he turned away from his wife and headed back to the house. "I'm going to take some Advil. Think

I'm coming down with the flu."

"Sorry. I'll be in shortly."

Jason spent the rest of the day lying around the house, popping pain relievers like jelly beans and dozing in front of the living room wide-screen. He was running a mild fever---anywhere from 99.8 to 100.4 degrees---and his muscles and ligaments felt like they were on fire at times, as if they were being stretched and torn apart while his body played tug-of-war with them. And the Advil didn't seem to be helping at all; whatever he was coming down with, he thought, it was going to be a doozy, if it wasn't already.

Cassie wasn't showing him much sympathy, either. She passed by him regularly as he lay stretched out on the couch, glancing his way, but rarely offering any words of comfort or solace. He almost felt as if they were complete strangers now, merely two ships passing in the night. Obviously, whatever was bothering her about him still held her tightly in its clutches, refusing to let go. Or, perhaps, she was the one who refused to let go…

Early that evening, as they picked at a simple dinner whose delicious aromas were wasted on Jason due to his ongoing distress, it started to rain, a light shower that, according to the local weatherman, would blossom into heavy thunderstorms overnight. Jason wondered how the downpour would affect their flourishing garden, and if he could expect a virtual tropical forest by sunrise.

Whatever the case, he promised himself he would peek at the plants before he left for work…or before he headed to the doctor's office.

Later, after downing a couple more Advils and a Benadryl for good measure, Jason turned in early for bed, hoping to get a good night's sleep. Cassie had wished him well, but declined to join him until after she had watched the late evening news. Lying beneath the covers, he prayed that his miserable situation would change significantly by tomorrow.

***

When the alarm buzzed early the next morning, Jason momentarily tugged himself out of his drugged sleep before Cassie slapped at the clock then slapped her hand across his forehead.

"You're not going anywhere right now, mister; you're still running a fever. Let me grab a shower, start getting ready for work, and I'll bring you some more Advil and take your temperature." She tucked him back under the covers then stepped over to the bathroom, shutting the door behind her.

But Jason couldn't go back to sleep; his whole body felt like there was something tearing and clawing at his skin just beneath the surface. Sweating, he struggled to a sitting position, thinking he'd never in his life felt this horrible being sick, and realized incongruously that he wasn't going to keep his promise about checking the garden before he set off for the doctor's office.

A minute later, as he edged over to the side of the bed, agony coursing through his body like electrical charges, the pain became unbearably acute, doubling him over. He pulled his shirt up to expose his stomach, wincing in torment and disbelief at what he saw. Countless green tendrils, lined with barbs and thorns, were poking and ripping through the surface of his skin, as if growing from within. Rivulets of blood trickled from each ragged wound. The tendrils were actually lengthening before his very eyes.

Sobbing and shouting for his wife, who probably couldn't hear him over the relentless drone of the shower, he pulled his boxers off only to discover even more emerald shoots piercing his thighs, their spikes and spines brutally coring his legs from the inside out. Likewise, he noticed scores of smaller tendrils puncturing his arms, blood leaking freely now, falling to the carpet like a grisly, red rain. And now his back felt as if it were on fire, as he imagined the tiny, budding shoots erupting from his neck to his buttocks.

His screams still falling on deaf ears, Jason now understood that Cassie had indeed found out about his brief affair at the office and, despite his dire situation, he mustered a weak grin over the fact that she had actually completed a task she had set out to do. Lastly, he knew that the seedlings he himself had planted in the barren square of their garden, and which Cassie and her mentor had never intended to grow outside, were for rose bushes.

The End.

Case #86540

William Rasmussen

William "Bill" Rasmussen was born in the state of Hawaii, well before the island even became a state. After a long career with the federal government as an FBI agent, during which time he worked in Honolulu, Hawaii, New York City and Memphis, TN, he retired in 2004.

Since late 2010, he has had well over a dozen short tales of horror published in both print and online magazines. His collection of short fiction, Claw Marks & Other Disturbing Diversions, was released in all digital formats in late 2010 by Crossroad Press; his novella, Infinity Twice Removed, co-written with Mike McBride, was released in hardcover and digital in December 2011 by Delirium Books. Both of these releases can be purchased from Amazon. He has two novelettes coming out later this summer as a two-story package trade paperback from Gallows Press.

Bill currently resides just outside of Memphis, TN, with his loving and supportive wife.

http://williamcrasmussen.wordpress.com/

CLAYTON HILL SANITARIUM

Ducky

Taylor Kingsbury

Murray hefted himself up onto one of the vacant seats lining the bar and set Ducky on the counter in front of the stool adjacent to his.

"This okay?" he asked Ducky. Satisfied by his companion's answer, Murray shifted his bottom, settling himself on his perch and getting comfortable.

Nick's Place was essentially deserted tonight, as it usually was on Wednesdays, and that was precisely why Wednesday was Murray's favorite night of the week to visit his favorite watering hole.

Tuesday was karaoke night, and this weekly ritual never failed to lure in a horde of scantily-clad sorority girls eager to warble their way through tuneless renditions of current Pop hits and desperately ironic odes to the guilty pleasures of yesteryear. This, in turn, lured in a horde of fraternity boys eager to continuously furnish these enthusiastic performers with dollar beers in the hopes of coaxing the lasses to become even more scantily-clad once their mundanely timeless and clumsy mating banter successfully convinced their vocalist of choice to accompany them to a less public location. Murray found the whole phenomenon distasteful. Certainly, he had done his share of skirt-chasing back when he was a young man, but in his day ladies still presented themselves like ladies and gentlemen still knew how to conduct themselves respectfully.

Thursdays were even worse. That was the night Nick's Place held their weekly Beer Pong tournaments, during which scores of overtly aggressive twenty-somethings piled into the pub to bask in the collective delusion that employing ping pong balls and plastic cups to force each other to consume an obscene amount of piss-grade ale somehow constituted a legitimate sporting event. All that grunting and hollering going on made it pretty impossible for a fella to just relax and enjoy a pint before calling it a night.

But Wednesday didn't have a gimmick. On this night of respite, Nick's Place was simply the best damn classic-rock-on-the-jukebox, peanut-shells-on-the-floor, smokem-iffyoo-gottem dive bar in town. It was a shithole, but it was Murray's kind of shithole, and on those pleasantly slow evenings, when he mounted a stool, folded his hands on the ash-strewn bartop, and let the musky bouquet
of stale cigarette smoke and stagnant spilled liquor waft up into his nostrils, it was like nestling into the embrace of a generously-bosomed lover.

Ducky preferred Wednesdays too, since the thin crowd meant that the likelihood of someone wandering over and making a fuss over him was reasonably slim. Ducky shared Murray's disposition, and the duo enjoyed the rare opportunities they were able to enjoy their beverages in peace without weathering the barrage of questions that Ducky's presence invariably solicited. After so many occasions of enduring nearly identical exchanges with a series of interchangeable strangers, Murray supposed he should be used to the curiosity he and his companion elicited, but he still found that trotting out the parade of rote answers he was so often impelled to provide was an annoying and often exhausting exercise.

Behind the bar, Sam gave Murray a nod while he finished stocking the cooler with the selection of imported bottled beers Nick's Place carried. Through conversation during his innumerable visits, Murray had gleaned that Sam owned the establishment in addition to tending bar there and that the only reason he hadn't changed the name to "Sam's Place" when he bought it several years back is because he didn't feel like paying for a new neon sign. Sam had purchased the bar from an Asian businessman named Yung and in fact had no idea who the electric blue "Nick's" on the sign referred to.

Sam slid the cooler closed and ambled over toward Murray, drying his hands on a dish towel that looked to be filthier than his hands could possibly ever be.

"Evenin', Murr," Sam croaked, his voice perpetually raw from the succession of cigarettes he sucked down throughout any given shift. He glanced over at Murray's sidekick and a wry half-smile tilted the corner of his mouth as he succumbed to Ducky's infectious grin. "Evenin', Ducky."

"Evening, Sam," Murray said. "What's good tonight?"

"Got something new you might like," Sam told him. "This double stout. Shit looks like soy sauce, you ask me, but I know you like the dark stuff. Supplier gave me a couple free kegs to try out. Give you one on the house if you want."

Murray's eyes twinkled whimsically. "Somethin' I learned in my years, you never turn down a free beer. Yessir, we'll give your double stout its day in court."

Sam motioned to Ducky. "Make it two?"

Murray looked over at his cohort and squinted his crow-clawed eyes thoughtfully. "You up for somethin' new, Ducky?"

Ducky didn't even bother answering. Murray already knew it was a dumb question, and he knew that Ducky knew he knew it. If Ducky was anything, he was a creature of habit.

"Naw, better just stick with the Coors Light for him," Murray told Sam.

Sam retrieved two mugs from the shelf behind him and filled them from the indicated taps, tilting the glasses expertly to allow the excess foam to sluice over the rims. Once the mugs were full he set the two beers down on the counter, the pale gold one in front of Ducky and one so dark that it looked like a glass of melted chocolate in front of Murray.

Murray grabbed the handle eagerly and clanged his glass against Ducky's.

"Cheers."

Murray took a long gulp of the stout, leaving a mouthful behind to slosh it around and savor the taste. Once he swallowed that down he sat there in silence for a moment, nodding his head while he let the finish tingle on his tongue.

"What'd you think?" Sam asked.

Murray's stubbled cheeks ceded to two plots of flesh ridged like wrinkled curtains as a broad smile spread across his face.

"What I think? I think you need to tell your supplier to bring down a couple more kegs, cause I maybe just switched brands, I'll tell you what."

"Glad you like it then," Sam said sincerely. "Well, I'll leave you boys to it. I'll keep an eye out, make sure those don't get empty." Sam went back to work, busying himself behind the counter, and Murray took out his smokes. He shook one loose from the softpack, gripped it between his lips, and set the pack down on the bar while his free hand fished through the pockets of his tattered jacket searching for a book of matches. He found what was he was looking for and struck a match absently, his routine fluid and effortless like routines become when you do them thousands and thousands of times. Once his cigarette was lit he cupped his fingers around the plastic ashtray closest to him and slid it over between him and Ducky. He let his eyes wander up to one of the TVs affixed to the wall behind the counter. Like always, the flatscreen was set to one of the sports channels. Murray watched the ticker at the bottom of the frame as it ran down the day's scores.

Ducky was just as interested as Murray was and he commented on the game they had been watching earlier that day.

"Uh-huh," Murray agreed. "You called it, all right. That deep bullpen they got, be amazed they don't make the Series this year, I'll tell you what."

A sudden commotion drew Murray's attention away from the television and he craned his head around to investigate. Off in one of the pub's darkened corners, an obese, unattractive woman was engaged in a heated one-sided argument with her apparent boyfriend, a gangly specimen who looked to be at least ten years younger than her and was so unnaturally skinny that his neck didn't look capable of supporting the weight of his pumpkin-shaped head. She easily outweighed him by two hundred pounds, so Murray could readily understand why the lad looked so terrified as she laid into him with a succession of shrill, yelping insults, her clenched, meaty fists and substantial arms gesticulating wildly in the air while she dished out her verbal assault. Murray couldn't make out her exact words—the squealing guitar solo of Boston's "More Than a Feeling" blaring from the jukebox effectively drowned her out—but there was no mistaking the sheer vigor of her prodigious scolding.

Never one to let such an inherently awkward moment pass without comment, Ducky tossed out one of his trademark snarky quips.

Murray couldn't stop himself from giggling. "Hot dog in a hallway?" he snickered conspiratorially. "Oh, man! I've got to remember that one, I'll tell you what!"

Since Murray was already looking around, he scanned the rest of the bar to note the other denizens. Other than Ducky and himself there were only five patrons in Nick's Place: the Hallway and the Hotdog, and a trio of college-aged guys seated around a table somewhere near the middle of the bar. Like Murray and Ducky the three twenty-somethings were doing their best to listen in on the squabble in the corner, obviously enjoying the floorshow as they cracked jokes amongst each other and worked towards polishing off the nearly empty pitcher of lager on their table.

Murray reclaimed his beer and took another deep pull from the mug as he went back to skimming the scores on the TV. He finished off his cigarette and mashed it out in the ashtray.

An unpleasant guffaw that resembled the braying of a donkey chimed out behind Murray, and it was loud enough to momentarily overshadow the music—the juke had moved on to Heart's "Barracuda." Then a booming proclamation roared across the room and even without turning around Murray could tell by the timbre that it was the same voice which had produced the ass-laughter.

"Hey! We need another pitcher here!"

Murray's eyes moved over toward Sam, who set down the glass he was wiping and glared at the rude beckoner, his infuriation barely masked by his cold, impassive face. Murray glanced back at the table where the three young men were sitting. The one who had issued the command was easy to spot; he was in the chair that directly faced the bar and he was holding his empty mug up in the air expectantly.

Without a word, Murray grabbed a pitcher and began occupying it from the tap. Once it was full, he slammed it down on the counter, producing a loud bang that echoed through the pub. The alcohol inhabiting the plastic carafe swayed inside of it like a lurching tide, waves of beer sloshing over the top as the liquid mass rocked back and forth.

"I'm not a waitress," Sam admonished. "I'm a bartender. You want a pitcher, you come get it at the bar."

Murray's eyes were still trained on the table as the three disrespectful youths burst into laughter. The song ended as if on cue, then the auto-play served up the relatively gentle "Ten Years Gone" by Led Zeppelin, providing a lull in the music that allowed Murray to plainly hear the ensuing conversation. The ruffian who had demanded the pitcher set down his glass and put up his hands submissively.

"It's cool, *sir*," he smirked, making the "sir" sound like an insult. "I'll meet you half way."

He rose from his chair and strode cockily toward the bar while his two buddies watched the scene unfold with admiring grins on their apelike faces. Sam was standing behind the counter and the pitcher like he was guarding both, his palms pressed against the bar so firmly that the intricate latticework of veins in his muscular forearms stood at attention.

As the young man approached the bar, Murray studied him intently. The kid was wearing a sleeveless gold Lakers jersey, the number "24" emblazoned on the chest in white numbers with purple trim. The flesh of his bare white shoulders was partially obscured by a plate of tattoos rendered in faded black ink. From his vantage point Murray could only clearly see the patterns etched onto the aggressively approaching lout's right arm. He noted a wide tribal band haloing around the pale bicep like an abstract drawing of barbed wire and, below that, a pair of crudely executed dice showing snake eyes.

"You should get a waitress," the Laker Fan continued, steadily stalking forward. "Hire one with big tits. Maybe you'd get more people coming in here."

If the kid was getting to Sam, the bartender certainly didn't show it. He stood statue still as the Laker Fan drew closer, his face flattened into a mask of restrained annoyance.

"You want tits, go to a strip club," Sam suggested. "You wanna drink this pitcher, you go back there with your friends and stop crackin' wise. Otherwise, you guys are done here."

The twenty-something nodded, but his lips were still pursed into a snotty grin.

"Yes, *sir*." That mocking tone again.

The Laker Fan picked the pitcher up off the bar and retreated to rejoin his group.

Ducky couldn't resist telling the guy what he thought of him. "Uh-huh," Murray tittered in agreement. "Total douchebag." "Ten Years Gone" hadn't quite built to its crescendo so Murray's voice resounded with unexpected clarity. Mortified, he covered his mouth with his hands. He looked over his shoulder cautiously, hoping that his words hadn't carried.

But they had.

The Laker Fan had nearly reached his friends but, hearing the remark, he paused immediately. He clumsily pounded the pitcher in his hand on the table, intending to quickly set it down but not quite getting the whole base of the carafe on the surface. His friends reacted swiftly, both of them reaching out to stop the plastic container from tumbling off the edge. They were largely successful but some of the beer roiled over the edge of the pitcher and splattered onto the floor.

But the Laker Fan wasn't paying any attention to that. He wheeled around and locked his vehement eyes on Murray, then started sauntering toward him slowly, his movements deliberate and malicious, like a cat sidling up behind an unsuspecting bird.

"What the fuck did you say?" the surly youth asked. Ducky starting mouthing off and, despite the gravity of the situation, Murray found himself laughing.

"Something funny?" the Laker Fan demanded, a deeper fury creeping into his voice.

Murray turned around on his stool to face the oncoming brute.

"No, no," Murray assured him. "Er… It's nothing."

But Ducky wouldn't let up. He was still muttering a string of biting jabs under his breath and Murray started giggling again.

"Something's obviously funny," the Laker Fan surmised, now coming even closer. "I want to know."

Murray fought the laughter away, but Ducky was still riffing so stifling it altogether was an impossibility.

"Quiet!" Murray whispered urgently over his shoulder. "Not now!"

The Laker Fan continued his methodical approach. "Come on, old man. What's funny?"

Ducky wanted Murray to tell him. But, then again, Ducky was far more fearless than Murray.

"You really want me to ask him that?" Murray chortled to Ducky.

Perplexed, the Laker Fan tilted his head to the side, but his face was still contorted in anger. The combination left him looking like a confused, testosterone-fueled puppy.

"Who are you talking to?"

"Okay," Murray agreed. "I'll tell him." He returned his attention to the Laker Fan, who had momentarily ceased his advance. "Ducky was just saying how lame your tattoos are. He said that tribal thing looks like something you picked by number off the wall of the tattoo parlor. And then, the dice? He was pointing out that snake eyes is the absolute worst roll you can get, so basically that tattoo is like advertising that you're a loser. Oh, and he also wanted me to ask you if you have a tramp stamp."

The Laker Fan was clearly taken aback. His mouth hung open stupidly, his rage momentarily suppressed by his astonishment.

Murray's eyes darted around nervously. Off to his side, Sam was still standing sentry behind the bar, but his imposing demeanor had softened and he was partaking in the hilarity that Murray was trying so hard to quell. Even the couple in the corner had ceased fire in their battle; both the Hotdog and the Hallway were bestowing their rapt attention on the exchange.

Ducky kept firing zingers and Murray was shuddering with nervous laughter.

"Oh, man!" Murray bellowed, delighted. "That's so funny! Stop though, seriously."

The Laker Fan glanced back at his friends, both of whom looked just as puzzled as he did. "Who are you talking to, old man?" he asked again, this time somewhat cautiously, the flummoxed look on his face now even more pronounced. "Am I missing something here?"

Ducky answered the question and Murray let out another burst of riotous glee.

"What?" the Laker Fan shouted. "What are you laughing at?"

Murray used his knuckles to rub the tears from the corners of his eyes. He was laughing so hard he could barely get the words out.

"Ducky says..." Murray had to pause as another convulsion of chuckles burbled out of him. "He says, yeah, you're missing something... About two steps on the evolutionary chart!" He slapped his knees with glee and somewhere behind him he heard Sam laughing ever louder than he was.

The Laker Fan just stood there, blinking.

And then he noticed Ducky sitting on the counter.

The Laker Fan skulked forward once again, but this time he wasn't walking toward Murray—his stare was fixated on Ducky. He shifted to his right, coming around the side of Murray's companion, completely absorbed as he took in each of his features.

His tiny, sleek body.

His vivid, glossy yellow skin.

The lumpy cluster atop his backside.

The two expressive, friendly eyes in the center of his smooth, rounded head, perpetually gleaming with warmth and mirth.

The vibrant orange expanse jutting out below those eyes, its two halves fused into a yawning, merry smile.

Ducky.

The Laker Fan's O-shaped mouth stretched into a beaming, bemused grin that bore a close resemblance to the one worn by the character sitting atop the counter.

"Holy shit!" the Laker Fan hooted, causing his friends to rise tentatively to their feet and crane their heads up, seeking a glimpse of the source of his exclamation. "This crazy old fuck's talking to a rubber ducky!"

Then he noticed the mug of beer situated in front of Ducky, nearly twice his size, towering over him like a glass monolith.

"Holy shit!" the Laker Fan howled again. "He has a beer!" He gestured excitedly at Murray. "Is that for him? For your duck?"

Murray chuckled knowingly. "Yeah, old Ducky loves his Coors Lights, that's for sure."

The Laker Fan erupted into a disconcerting laughter that swerved perilously close to hysteria. Finally grasping the scene, his friends joined him, overpowering the bridge of "Ten Years Gone" with their own hyena-like chorus.

"Wait! Wait! So, you buy beer for your rubber duck?"

"Well sure," Murray said matter-of-factly. "That's what friends do. He'll get the next round."

This brought about another raucous eruption and the cackling choir reached a fever pitch. Now it was the Laker Fan's turn to smudge away moisture from his eyes.

As for Murray and Ducky, they were starting to get a bit exasperated. This was veering into familiar territory for them. "He's your friend, huh?" the Laker Fan wanted to know.

"That's right, son. Ducky here is my best friend in the world." Murray glanced over at Ducky and beamed at him affectionately. As always, Ducky was smiling right back.

"And you talk to him?"

Murray shrugged. "Of course I do."

"And your rubber duck talks back to you?"

"You kidding me? I can't get him to shut up most of the time." Murray gave Ducky a wink.

"Why isn't he talking now, then?"

"I reckon because he doesn't want to talk to you." "He doesn't, huh?"

"Well, he ain't. So I reckon he doesn't."

Murray noticed that Sam had tensed up again and he knew the bartender was ready to step in if things got ugly. Even though Ducky certainly had enough spunk for the both of them, it reassured Murray a bit to know that he had a slightly larger ally on hand as well.

"That's too bad," the Laker Fan lamented mockingly. "Well, listen, maybe it's just because he don't know me that well. Maybe if I picked him up…"

"That's not a good idea, son," Murray interrupted him sternly.

"Why's that?"

"Because he wouldn't like that at all. And I wouldn't want to see you get hurt."

The Laker Fan's two friends were now standing erect and they shifted on their heels as if getting ready to move forward. Seeing this, the tattooed youth waved them off.

"It's fine. I got this."

The song kicked into its booming finale. Murray noted that the Hotdog and the Hallway were still watching them, but the music was now likely too loud for them to hear what was being said.

"Come on, old man," the Laker Fan insisted. "Let me hold him. Just for a minute."

"Young man, I said no." The playfulness in Murray's voice was a distant memory now, replaced by a dire sincerity.

"You gonna hurt me if I pick your duck up?" "It's not me you gotta worry about, kid."

The young man's hand was resting on the counter, his palm slowly sliding across the bar, shifting closer to Ducky. There was a malevolent twinkle in his eyes.

"Then what should I be worried about?"

Murray ran a hand through his unkempt silver mane and let out a deep breath.

"Let's just say the last fella who tried it didn't have a very good day," Murray intoned gravely.

The Laker Fan raised his eyebrows dramatically, his hand inching ever closer, his fingers almost touching Ducky's rump.

"Yeah? What happened to him?"

"It wasn't pretty," Murray assured him. His eyes wandered down as he summoned the memory. "We was at a park, Ducky and me. It was a real nice day out. We were just sittin' on a bench there, reading, enjoying the afternoon."

Murray's eyes darted back up, locking on the cruel, gleaming beads above the Laker Fan's insincere smile.

"Then this kid comes up to us," Murray continued. "Kid about your age. Had the same kind of tattoos even, actually. He starts asking us questions, pretty much the same ones you've been asking. Same kind of attitude. Gets around to, 'Can I hold him?' I tell him no, he can't. And all the while, Ducky's telling me to warn this kid. Sayin' if this kid so much as touches him, there's going to be trouble. So I tell the kid, like I'm telling you now…"

Murray glanced over at the Laker Fan's hand on the bartop. His fingers were pattering lightly against the wood, digits dancing mere inches away from Ducky.

"But he doesn't listen, and he grabs Ducky…"

The Laker Fan's wolfish grin widened, his fingers tapping more insistently on the counter.

"And what did Ducky do?" he wondered disdainfully.

Murray rubbed his craggy chin reflectively.

"First thing he did was bite two of the kid's fingers off…" The Laker Fan's digits paused their whimsical wiggling.

The impenetrable, oil-black smile halving Ducky's waxy beak glistened in the bar light.

"The kid starts screamin' and hollerin'," Murray went on. "Blood just gushing all over the place. I never seen so much blood in my life. Problem is, the kid starts panicking, and his hand tightens up. The three fingers he had left, I mean. And he ends up squeezing Ducky tighter. Ducky didn't like that one bit, I'll tell you what."

Murray absently reached over and slid a cigarette out of his softpack. It only took him a second to get it lit. Enthralled in the tale, the Laker Fan didn't stir. Murray took a deep drag and exhaled a thick cloud of acrid smoke before continuing his story.

"So Ducky jumps out of the kid's hand and latches onto his face. Starts gnawing away. And the kid's just yelpin' now, like some kind of wounded animal. He's reaching up to pull Ducky off, but Ducky's little beak is clamped on tight. And these two stumps on the kid's hand are just shooting blood up in the air, like two geysers goin' off."

Murray took another hit off his cigarette.

"Finally, the kid goes down. I think he passed out, losing all that blood. So Ducky let's go and I scoop him up and get him out of there fast as I can. And Ducky's swearin' it's not his fault, and I know he's right, because we warned the kid. I just got a quick look, but it was easy to see what Ducky done to him. You couldn't miss it. His nose was clean tore off his face."

Murray mimed the action on his own nose to illustrate. "There was just this nubby wad of… meat. Hangin' off to the side there. Kid's whole face was covered in blood. And right in the middle of all that, this huge gaping hole you could see inside. Just a big bloody pit where his nose used to be. Like I said, a little bit of somethin' hanging loose there. Like someone took a bite of some steak, chewed it up and spit it back out. I reckon Ducky swallowed the rest."

The Laker Fan's face was taut with skepticism but it was clear he was struggling to keep his self-satisfied smile in place.

Murray sucked on his smoke once more, then presented the moral of the story.

"Don't get me wrong," he said, his voice a bit more chipper now that he had gotten past the more unsavory parts of the narrative. "Like I said, Ducky's my best friend. I never had a better one. I have more fun with him than anyone else, and if I had to choose, I'd say I've never known a finer fella, I'll tell you what."

Murray squinted, a sea of wrinkles expanding across his brow as his eyes went steely.

"But Ducky don't like you, young man. So I'm sayin' to you, just like I said to that kid in the park that day, you're better off just leavin' him be."

The Laker Fan's skin was pallid and a discernible film of sweat had formed on his forehead. He chortled derisively, still trying to maintain his cock-sure mien, but it was obvious that his heart wasn't in it anymore.

"You're fucking crazy. You know that, old man?" "We got a difference of opinion on that one, son."

The song ended and Nick's Place was suddenly populated by a punctuating, oppressive silence while the juke box searched for its next selection. Murray and the Laker Fan appraised each other soberly in that brief moment when the world seemed to stand still just for them.

It was Murray who broke the mute stalemate.

"Question you gotta ask yourself is, how bad do you wanna find out?"

An unmistakable chiming guitar riff split through the silence and consumed the atmosphere, announcing the opening salvo of Blue Oyster Cult's "(Don't Fear) The Reaper."

The Laker Fan juddered as an anxious chuckle prattled out of him. Murray watched him slowly shift his hand across the bar, this time moving his fingers away from Ducky until they slid over the edge of the counter and curled up into a fist at his side.

"You and your friend enjoy your beers." The Laker Fan sneered dismissively, shot one last look down at Ducky, then returned to his table to rejoin his friends.

Murray didn't pay any further attention to the twenty-something trio. It wasn't until he finished his beer and got up from his stool that he realized they had quietly fled Nick's Place, leaving behind their untouched second pitcher and a pile of crumpled bills on the table that looked to be enough to account for their bill plus a wildly substantial tip.

Sam watched Murray swallow down the last gulp of his beer and he already had a fresh mug in hand, ready and waiting to provide a refill.

"Get ya another?" Sam offered.

Murray thought about it for a second, then shook his head. "Nah, I'm fine. That double stout was real good though. What do we owe you?"

Sam set the unused glass down and wagged his hand. "I've got you and Ducky covered tonight."

"That's real nice of you, Sam. Thanks. Somethin' for yourself then."

Murray dug a five-dollar bill out of his pants pocket and flattened it out on the counter. He picked Ducky up off the bar, cradling the tiny yellow torso in the palm of his hand.

"We'll see you real soon."

"Anytime, Murr. You and Ducky have yourselves a good night."

Murray smiled. As usual, Ducky was smiling too. "We always do."

Murray gave a quick wave then tucked Ducky against his side and carefully navigated his way to the entrance, limping a bit as his brittle legs carried him and his comrade out into the still, humid night.

Just outside, Murray paused in front of the door to light a cigarette, taking special care not to burn Ducky with the match.

"That was some night, wasn't it, Ducky? I didn't get a good feeling from that kid; I'll tell you what. Somethin' tells me he wasn't all there upstairs. Bit loco, know what I mean?"

"Fuck him," Ducky said. "Let's go get some tacos." And so they did.

The End.

Case #88339

Taylor Kingsbury

Taylor Kingsbury is an author, radio personality, screenwriter, musician, and award-winning pop culture columnist. His debut short story anthology, *Les Fables*, was released in 2011. Taylor is currently working on his first novel as well as putting the final copy-editing touches on the tales which will appear in the follow-up to *Les Fables*. He earned his MA in Creative Writing from Claremont Graduate University in 2012.

In addition to his macabre literary pursuits, Taylor hosts the popular weekly metal radio show "Touch Of Evil" (www.kspc.org) and scribes a music blog, "Life On A Shelf" (lifeonashelf.tumblr.com). He lives in southern California with his fish, Mephistopheles. Contact Taylor at happyendingrocks@hotmail.com

CLAYTON HILL SANITARIUM

The Crevice

Ryan Link

Physician: Dr. Peterson
9268-WCT29

In my youth, I had a penchant for reckless behavior. So reckless, in fact, that I willfully agreed to tie myself to another man and descend through a small hole in the earth. I cringe now, looking back through the lens of learned caution, but at the time, carelessness came naturally. Neither my friend Willis nor I once considered the physical danger of such an inane activity, much less the reality of what we would experience.

The hole we were to descend was located on my uncle's property in the eastern reaches of the Texas hill country. The front half of his land--as we took to calling it--was green and peppered with old oaks. Cattle ambled about from pasture to pasture, munching and ruminating and swatting at flies.

The back half of the property, however, was much too rocky for bovine tastes. As a result, it was unimproved and largely untrodden. It was in this region that Willis and I chanced across a shallow, dry ravine--not unusual in this part of the state, though I had never seen this particular one. It was about a man's height in depth, fifty or so feet in length, and was bordered with mesquite brush. Grey rock pushed through a thin skin of dirt and roots in irregular intervals along its walls.

Willis spotted the opening first. It appeared initially to be little more than a fissure in the rock, running horizontally at the base of the western ravine wall. The fissure widened, though, as we brushed away the detritus that shrouded it. A crevice soon opened before us, just wide enough for a man to squirm through without much discomfort. Cool air flowed freely out of the hole, suggesting more lay beyond.

We noticed crude markings carved into the bordering rock as we continued to clear the area from debris. Most of the carvings amounted to little more than simple X's, but one in particular, we both agreed, resembled the face of a rat. I tried, through various contortions, to see beyond the opening, but only met with darkness. Our interest was piqued, but the day was fading, and we had no equipment to support a dive underground. We left the site, resolved to return in the morning prepared for a descent.

That evening we readied ourselves, though the preparations were cursory at best: a nylon rope, three spools of five hundred feet of string, three flashlights, and a .22 caliber rifle fixed with a homemade shoulder strap. Later, as night fell, we opened a bottle of scotch and took to drinking. Sleep found us early, as did dawn.

***

We set out for the ravine as the first full rays of sun spread out over the pastures. Grasshoppers buzzed and fled from our feet as we walked through the feathery grass. Cows ceased their chewing and watched us with detachment. Their eyes followed us, dark marbles in crescents of white.

"Those damn things always make me edgy," Willis said, nodding toward the herd. The legs of his jeans were wet with morning dew. "They're too dumb to trust."

"Kind of like you?" I asked. Willis chortled and shook his head. Upon arrival at the crevice, I attempted again to see beyond the

opening, this time armed with flashlights. The passage sloped downward at a shallow angle to the limit of my vision, only widening slightly. "Hello!" I called out into the opening. We both laughed.

The thinner of the pair, I volunteered to scout the hole first. Willis secured himself to one end of the nylon rope and held the other out for me to do the same. Once joined, I chambered a round in the rifle, satisfied by the sound of the sliding metal parts. Willis looked at me with upraised eyebrows. A smile broke over my face as I jiggled the flashlight that I had taped to the muzzle. I fed the gun in before me and lowered myself, head first, down the crevice. The fit was tight, but I had room to breathe and crawl. My eyes slowly adjusted to the loss of sunlight as I squirmed into the hole up to my feet. Cool, earthy air flowed around me.

"What do you see?" Willis called after me.

I shone the light down the passage. "Not much, but it seems to widen quite a bit just ahead," I replied. I wriggled further through the passage. The walls were rough against my skin, and dirt clumped in my eyes. A thick brown roach turned and scurried away at my approach.

"What now?" Willis called down.

"I'm getting there!" At around the twenty-foot mark, the passage widened significantly in all directions. I was able to stand in a crouch.

"It's a lot wider!" I cried back. "Come through! I can stand!" I chuckled at the sound of Willis squeezing through the opening at the surface. The walls of the passage around me crawled with angry roaches, indignant at the sweeping beams of light. Ahead, the passage widened even more. It continued down at a shallow angle for a distance, and then curved off to the right. I waited in the cool air for Willis, listening to the sound of a thousand small limbs.

He arrived, panting and covered in dark brown dirt. The spool of string in his hand was already unraveling line. We untied the large rope, wound it, and Willis slung it over his shoulder. I kept the rifle ready.

"Shall we?" I asked, motioning ahead. Willis nodded. We crept forward, able to stand a bit more with each step. Eddies of dry dirt swirled around our feet. Once we neared the right turn, we were fully upright and could move at a walking pace. The number of roaches had decreased, though I could still hear them scurrying behind us.

After the bend, the passage opened up into a room, about twenty feet cubed. There were no recognizable cave features or sparking crystals of any sort, only grey rock walls, rubble, and the dried-out husk of an armadillo. We sat and rested for a moment, even venturing to turn out all of the flashlights. The darkness was complete; a few seconds was enough.

The passage continued on from the room at a reduced width. Willis and I were forced to walk single-file between the ragged walls; I was in front with the gun, and Willis followed with the second flashlight.

"Look, it's changing color," Willis said, shining the light upwards. The ceiling was taking on a much darker tone, almost sooty, as if a giant candle had been burning beneath it for ages.

As I was gazing roof-wards, a metallic clink sounded from my shuffling feet. I stepped back, shining the gun-light at the ground. A dull yellow object reflected in the dust and rocks on the cave floor. I bent over and blew at the ground to clear it. Six spent brass ammunition cartridges lay spread out around us.

"Those are revolver rounds," Willis observed, kneeling down next to me. He picked one up and inspected it. "They're old, too, by the looks of them – real old. 44-40." He shone the light back the way we had come, looking for more. Again, a bit of brass revealed itself. A few feet back, we found two unspent cartridges. We both squatted down and stared at them for a minute.

"Someone dropped them," I offered.

"Why would someone be shooting down here anyway?" he asked.

I thought for a moment. "Well, _we_ brought a gun."

Willis kept staring at the unspent rounds. A drop of sweat trickled down the bridge of his nose and fell to the floor, staining the dirt. Abruptly, he stood and strode ahead down the passage past the empty cartridges, shining the light on the walls.

"Here, look," he said, pointing along the wall. "You can see where one hit and grazed off."

He traced his finger along a chalky strip that was cut out of the dark rock at eye level.

"I wonder what they were shooting at," I said, pointing the light in the direction we had yet to travel. My brow creased. "A coyote?"

Willis snorted. "No, coyotes won't come down this far." We stood, unmoving for many seconds. I kept the light pointed deeper into the passageway. The walls and floor descended into an orb of darkness.

"Well?" Willis urged at last.

I nodded once and stepped forward down the passage.

"Hold on," Willis said from behind. "The string is done. That's five hundred feet." I turned and shone the light on his grinning face. He was busy extracting the next spool from his satchel and tying it on.

As we descended, the incline became increasingly more pronounced, and the temperature rose. The cool flow ceased, and the air became thick with stagnation. At times, the passage was piled waist-high with debris, and at one point the floor dropped abruptly by a couple of feet. After this drop, we again linked ourselves with the rope, though it would have availed us little in the worst case.

Deeper, the cave crickets became numerous, and we slowed to look at them. They shone pale against the ceiling, which had turned completely black. The insects cast disturbing shadows many times their own size, dark misshapen lobsters clinging to the walls.

"We need an exterminator," Willis said. I laughed, but it seemed odd that insects were so plentiful this far from the surface. We carried on, a little plug of light in a dark tube.

It was when we stopped to tie on the final spool of string, that we first heard it. A deep sound drifted from the passage ahead. We froze and listened. At first it sounded like a distant rumbling or even thunder, but then we made out something akin to laughter. I clutched the gun and looked at Willis with wide eyes. He stared toward the noise, his mouth gaping.

We heard the sound again; this time it was unmistakable. Willis snapped his head toward me and grabbed my arm. His lips had lost all color, and the hair on his arms stood raised. I took a step backwards.

"Wait," he said, relaxing slightly. "We must be near an opening. The other end of the cave must be ahead."

I thought for a moment. "No. We've been heading downwards the whole time. We are probably three or four hundred feet deep." I looked back the way we had come. The trail of our footprints carried off into the darkness.

"Then there's a shaft or some kind of opening to the surface," Willis said. "It must be carrying the sound down here."

I considered his explanation, but I was unconvinced. Willis began attaching the new spool of string. I pressed my ear against the hard wall, but the silence of the rock was absolute. The final spool was ready, and Willis looked at me with shrugged shoulders. I turned ahead and carried on, still gripping the rifle.

Our footfalls rang dully against the walls, and the sound of our breathing seemed abnormally loud in such a silent world. We stopped every minute or so to listen again for the laughing noise, but heard nothing. Ahead, the passage split into two. We stood at the fork considering our path, but the openings were identical. We chose the left one.

After another few minutes of walking the passage widened around us into a long open room that gradually curved to the left. A trickle of water dripped down the near wall to our right. I shone my light on it and moved closer for inspection. The water was dark. I touched it and examined the liquid on my finger, surprised by its warmth. It was deep brown and thick, like engine oil. A shining black millipede scurried through the wet stain on the rock.

"Hey, Willis, look at...," I began to say but was cut off by a reverberating laughter from the far end of the room, beyond where we could see. I froze and crouched to the floor in terror. "Shut your light off!" I whispered as I reached toward the muzzle of the rifle to extinguish my own flashlight. Willis fumbled to turn his off. He finally succeeded and cast us into darkness. My vision burned with the phantom image of the flashlight beams.

The laughter slowly died out, but it was replaced by deep slurping speech. There were two distinct voices, both low and ponderous. I jumped as Willis reached out and found my trembling wrist. He crept close to me, scraping against the floor.

"What the holy hell is that!?" he whispered.

My throat was constricted and my breathing was shallow and rapid. I did not answer. My eyes began to water as we lay there in the dirt.

Suddenly, Wilson shifted and turned on his flashlight, covering the aperture with his hand. A red glow spilled over us. He stood up, crouched, and began to creep forward towards the voices. I reached out to grab his ankle, but he was already too far away.

"What are you doing?" I croaked. "Turn it off!" I realized we were still attached with the rope, and I quickly untied myself.

Willis kept moving, slowly shuffling forward. I watched his glowing hand recede into the long room.

"Damn it," I said to myself. I stumbled to my feet and scrambled after him, uncertain of my steps. Just as I reached him, the laughter shook us again. It was horribly loud, echoing in my chest. Willis switched off his light. For a moment we were plunged again into darkness, but soon our eyes adjusted, revealing a new horror. Ahead, the room bent sharply to the left, and a dim flickering light bathed the ground near the curve as well as the far-right wall. Something--a fire, perhaps--was burning beyond the bend.

The voices spoke again. I could make out words and intonations, but the language was guttural, wet and terrifying. Vowels and consonants bled together with hideous sloshing sounds. I realized after a moment, that a shadow was visible against the far-right wall. The shape was moving in synch with the speech; it was the shadow of the speaker, gesturing and breathing. The form was huge and distorted against the flickering light. I grabbed onto Willis, but he kept moving forward.

I stared at the shadow as we crept ever closer. It seemed, briefly, to sharpen and I saw what I thought to be a head of some kind set atop a hulking body. My legs stopped, and I let go of Willis. His dim silhouette trembled in front of the flickering yellow glow as he moved away. We both dropped to the floor when a tiny figure appeared, peeking out from the nearly right angle of the adjacent left wall.

I only saw shadow. The form was at most three feet tall. The head was humanlike, but the ears were large, like a rodent's, and each tapered to a sharp point above the skull. It crept out from the corner silently. The form walked, much like a chimpanzee, on two short hind legs and two longer upper limbs. The creature stopped and craned its head toward Willis as if it were trying to make out fine details in the dark.

Then, the beast was illuminated. Willis had turned his flashlight on and was pointing it at the creature. I opened my mouth in a silent cry. Its skin was grey, smooth, and nude except for a white patch of hair on each of its forearms. It had large triangular eyes set in a head that was wide at the top but tapered to a small, lipless mouth. It seemed to be grinning. Again, the two voices boomed in laughter.

The tiny creature began to hobble forward on all fours toward Willis. I could not scream, nor even bring myself to whisper. I pointed my rifle at the little horror, but the muzzle shook wildly. Willis followed the creature with the light as it slowly approached him.

The being stopped near Willis and held up a long-clawed hand. Willis turned his head to me, keeping the light positioned on the creature. His eyes were wide, but he seemed more astonished than frightened. With the smooth motion of a geared mechanism, his head spun back around to face the abomination in front of him.

I choked on my own breath as he reached out and grasped the wretched fingers.

Willis let his flashlight hand drop to his side such that the light pointed towards the floor. The room became darker as the light pooled on the ground. I watched Willis' illuminated feet step gingerly to the sharp corner. He paused. The creature seemed to be tugging at him to carry on past the threshold. Slowly, Willis peeked around the corner and down the passage toward the flickering light and the source of the voices.

Almost instantly, he screamed. I had never before, nor have I ever since, heard a man emit such a sound. He tore away from the creature, shrieking again, this time in physical pain. I stood and fired my flashlight.

"Here! Here!" I called out.

Against the illuminated right wall, I saw the shadow cast by the horrendous form shifting in alarm. Deep cries of warning rang out. Willis ran towards me, his face contorted in terror. I too turned and ran.

"Untie the rope!" I screamed. Willis was still trailing the rope we had used to link ourselves together. He pushed the rope down off of his body as he ran, nearly tripping. We reached the entrance to the long room at the same time. I pushed Willis into the narrow passage.

"Go!" I cried.

Just before entering the passage myself, I turned the rifle back into the room. The little horror was creeping towards us. A sly expression covered its face. Behind it, giant grey forms surged in the gloom. Huge limbs or trunks or tentacles of some sort filled the far end of the chamber.

I plunged into the passage as enormous noises erupted around me. We ran. Willis moaned in piteous, breathless terror. Sweat poured from my body. We scrambled over debris and slammed repeatedly into the narrow side walls, twisting ourselves as we fled. At intervals I would turn and shine the light behind us, but I saw nothing. Gradually, Willis began to slow down, despite my constant prodding.

When we reached the open space housing the armadillo, Willis fell. Something skidded along the floor in front of him. I stumbled over Willis and collapsed to my hands and knees. Just ahead, I saw the object that had sent Willis sprawling: a six-shot revolver, dirty and tarnished. A plume of dust circled around it. We were not the first to flee wildly from the depths of this cave.

Behind me, Willis cried out from the ground in pain. I rushed over to him. He was shining his light on his left arm, which had been torn by the creature as he had pulled away. He was bleeding, but the wound appeared superficial.

"Come on! A few hundred feet," I said, tugging at his collar. Willis managed to stand and started moving forward again. I was relieved, but my guts clenched as I saw the little grey beast emerge into the room. The way was too small for the hulking forms to have followed but the tiny creature must have slipped easily through the passages. I pulled Willis and we hurried ahead.

Soon we were forced onto all fours. Most of the roaches scurried away, but some squished under my hands. I knew we were nearing the entrance. Willis scrambled ahead, grunting and gasping. I turned back just as he was entering the section of passage through which we would have to crawl on our bellies. The creature was feet behind. I fired the gun twice, to a pair of deafening cracks. Either I missed, or the bullets did no harm to the creature, as it continued to creep forward. Wriggling, I pushed on towards the sound of Willis' labored breathing. I do not remember the crawl to the surface.

Suddenly, I emerged into daylight. Willis was yelling something and pulling me by the arms. With a final heave, I was free. I turned on the ground, fell to my side, and fired the remaining rounds into the crevice. I quickly stood and raised the rifle as a club, expecting a grey clawed hand to emerge. But it never did.

Slowly, the world around me bled into my consciousness. Willis was lying prostrate on the floor of the ravine, covered in filth and blood. He was unconscious. I took off my shirt and wound it around his arm, tying it tightly.

"Willis," I urged. "Willis."

He stirred. "Huh?"

"Willis, listen to me," I said. "We have to block it up." "Block it up?" he asked, his eyes trying to focus.

"The opening--the crevice," I said, looking back at the hole.

"Yes," he said, rising unsteadily to his feet.

Over the next few minutes, we gathered the largest free stones we could find. I wedged the biggest of these into the crevice and filled the gaps with the smaller ones. I pounded the mass of rocks with the butt of the rifle to seal them in and covered it all with dirt and leaves. Once satisfied, I looked at Willis. We were caked in sweat and breathing heavily.

"No one can know," I said. I put my hands on my knees and tried to catch my breath. "No one can ever go down there."

Willis stared at me vacantly. His chin was trembling. I stepped towards him and shook him by the shoulders.

"No one!" I said. "No one! Do you hear!?" Willis nodded.

***

The infection nearly killed him. He suffered in the hospital for over a week, wracked with blood poisoning. I lied about how he got the wound, even to his parents. I wondered, as Willis lay there in fits of fever, what I would say if he were to die; would I tell it true then? Luckily, on the ninth day, his fever broke, and the wound dried up, and I never had to answer.

While he was recovering, Willis and I spoke at night after everyone had gone about what had happened below the earth. He was quite willing to discuss the small creature--eager even. It seemed he had developed some kind of affinity for the beast, despite his protestations to the contrary. However, Willis flatly refused to speak of the gargantuan beings. At the mention of them, he would turn pale and his forehead would sweat, and he would descend into a brooding silence. So, I let him be.

***

A year later, I fell out of contact with Willis when he moved to California with his new bride, Carol. The wedding was the last time I saw him. Willis and I spoke on the phone a few times, but distance inevitably put our friendship on hiatus. He seemed happy during our last conversation, though. He said he was putting the whole ordeal in the past and urged me to do the same.

I tried, but in the years that followed, I was haunted with thoughts of what we had seen. My sleep suffered, especially. When I did sleep, I dreamt of the horror I had witnessed. I would wake in the night in fits, sweating and gripping the sheets, kicking at the little creature with grey hands. On occasion, I thought about telling someone in hopes it would help, but I never did. I always remembered what Willis and I had agreed. Eventually, time carried me far enough from the trip down the crevice that I could manage a day or two without thinking of it.

Then, years of forgetting were erased with a single call from Carol. She sounded frail and broken, and I knew immediately that something was wrong. My first thought was that Willis had died, but Carol told of something worse.

In the night, Carol would find him at his desk frantically sketching, pressing down with frightening force into the paper beneath. At first, he had been unresponsive, fully ignoring any attempt to divert him. But after a time, he had become vicious towards her as he drew and had even struck her on a number of occasions.

The images he produced, however, were more upsetting than the physical aggression. The vast majority of his drawings were of a small being--a "monkey" as Carol put it--with large triangular eyes, furry arms, and the ears of a rat. She mentioned other images too, but would not describe their nature. She said only that they were horrible and refused to burden me with a description, claiming that I would never forgive her if she did.

But there was more to tell beyond just the drawing obsession. Willis had taken to incessantly clawing at his left arm, both waking and in his sleep. He constantly complained of a deep itching beneath his scars, an aggravation he could not reach. Twice, Carol had been forced to rush him to the hospital, fearing he had severed a major vein in his fits of scratching. Willis had recovered from both incidents, but his forearm was always raw and peeling from constant irritation.

When, finally, I asked to speak with Willis himself, the true cause of our conversation surfaced. Willis had vanished. Carol had last seen him one week prior. His car and all of his belongings were still at the house. He had taken nothing with him but his wallet and the clothes he had been wearing. She hoped that, maybe,

I would have something to offer--some bit of his past that may explain it all.

I lied.

Carol made me promise that I would call her back if anything came to mind, and we said a sad goodbye. I could scarcely set the phone in its cradle before I fell to my knees. His wife would never know--she could not. But I had to be certain.

***

I looked out at the pastures, squinting in the noon sun. They were empty; the cattle had been sold. The grass was brown and crunched under my feet. I rested for a moment under the shade of one of the big oaks, but soon carried on.

As I approached the crevice, I sighed with sick resignation. The rocks that I had sealed it with years before were scattered, and the opening yawned up at me. "Willis," I said looking up to the sky. Tears welled in my eyes.

Slowly, I began to place the stones back over the crevice, wedging them in with the heel of my boot.

The End.

Case #43063

Ryan Link

Ryan is a native Texan who lives in Houston with his wife of ten years. He works as an analyst and programmer in the wind energy industry and holds a Ph. D. in mechanical engineering from the University of Houston. Writing is a new interest of his, but he plans to pursue it fervently going forward. Some of his favorite authors and influences are Frank Herbert, Alastair Reynolds, George R. R. Martin, and H. P. Lovecraft.

Dark Verse

Physician: Dr. Salam
7128-DV7SSJJ

Leo Norman
Joseph Robert Villari
Michael Pendragon

1. Bitten

The night the electricity cut out
I reached for a torch, a candle,
To light the way through the dark
To the dunny
But came up empty except for a tea light-
Timid and weak.
It threw its light to the corners
Where it fought with the darkness
And lost.
The stragglers came back,
Wounded, staggering, crying for help,
Telling tales of monsters
That lived in cupboards, under beds, Or
lurked in the shadows.

I stepped out into the night alone.

I was shaking worse than the tongue
Of the flame, than the wagging finger
Of mother or, worse, of the wife
Had she known it, seen it, foretold it.
The truth is I knew you were there:
Long black hair, slender, asleep in your lair.
I looked down with my familiar
Thousand-yard stare
until slowly you stirred,
came into focus
and glared
to think that I'd dared
and drew back and bared
your pearly white fangs.

It wasn't my fault

I muttered, rubbing the wound,
Salving my conscience,
That she hadn't cared.
Hadn't she cared?
After all that we'd shared…

2. Transformation

   I felt the first stirrings as the moon waxed,
And knew at once that I'd begun to change
My chest grew tense, tighter and then relaxed
The man in the mirror seemed thin and strange
He stopped shaving, started ranting, raving
Let his nails grow long, sharpened them to points
Scratched his mark on walls, on floors, on paving
He worked out hard, bulked up and stretched his joints
But he, of course, was me, I think, I thought
A stranger in my house, my clothes, my head
And in the end the past it meant for nought
As all that came before soon wound up dead
The 'ow' of pain became my fav'rite vowel
I'd prowl for victims in the night, then howl.

3. Silver Bullet

I had transformed
completely
when the end finally came

My muzzle panted
steaming
hot breath as the moon waned

My big green eyes
gleamed
at the thought of fresh meat

My dripping fangs
shone white

in my hunter's jaw

But the truth came like a bullet
And ripped me in half
Gripped at my heart
As I stood in the silvery light
of her growing full moon.

I squirmed under her eyes,
Wriggled and scratched at my fur,
Stepped out of my hide,
Realised it was her
I'd denied when part of me died I'd
been less than a man

No wolf, but a dog.

Case #19947

Leo Norman

Leo Norman is a writer and teacher. He often writes about monsters because he knows they are a part of us. Leo lives in England with his wife and son.

Deep in the pit
Where myriad eyes in madness stare
And Indian lies swell with despair
Where true love dies as lovers share
Illicit kisses dark and warm
Wrapped in the arms of sin
Where every sigh takes mortal form
And anguished cries like hornets swarm
Screams scorch the skies, a fiery storm
Arises from within
Caught in the pit
Where demon spears impale the dead
And midnight fears run thick and red
Where all the tears you've ever shed
Lie spread before wrought iron chains
And wash the prison floor
While madmen howl like quartered thanes
The Reaper's cowl hides mortal stains
His bony scowl all that remains
For those who've 'gone before' Lost

in the pit

Where laughter rings with hollow mirth And
solitude brings sorrow's dearth 'Til curséd
beings condemn their birth Entreat the stars
their torments end And dodge the devil's
prod
Tho scorned and flayed the dead unbend
Their bodies bowed, yet proud they wend
As unafraid their souls ascend
To curse the hand of God

Michael Pendragon

Michael Pendragon grew up in the pine barrens of rural southern New Jersey and several of his short stories reflect his early experiences there. After graduating high school, he briefly served in the U.S. Navy in Orlando, Florida. He later worked a variety of jobs including salesman, security guard, short order cook, cashier, construction worker, telemarketer, dishwasher, baker, administrative assistant, and assistant editor for a New York City-based publishing company. He began his literary career at Jersey City State University where he wrote for the school paper, "The Gothic Times," and edited their art and literary magazine "Excalibur."

His fictional works are primarily of the horror genre, and his poetry primarily in a (dark) Romantic vein. His writings have appeared in over 100 publications, including: "Ocular," "The Dream Zone," "Event Horizon," "Pluto's Orchard," "The Romantics Quarterly," "The Catbird Seat," "The Blue Lady," "The Roswell Literary Review," "Frisson," "Voyage," "Mindmares," "Nasty Piece of Work," "Monomyth," "The Raintown Review," "Enigmatic Tales," "Morbid Curiosity," "Lovecraft's Mystery Magazine," "Terror Tales," "The Scarlet Literary Magazine," and "Masque Noir." Several of his poems are currently featured in the Fall 2013 issue of "The Horror Zine Magazine."

CLAYTON HILL SANITARIUM

Trees alit with flame
Acrid was the air
Fire as absent as meaning
There is no fire, this man said
It is no more than a change of seasons
This man said
Extinguished with our dreams
The ones we made
The ones we made, they were extinguished
The teeth, how they click and snip
You can hear the clacking of their jaws, he said
Skeletons of midnight and mud
Can you hear them clack
Flesh to mud and muck and mire
There is a purpose here, he said
Can you handle it, he asked
Are their worlds beyond, I asked
All said, all cackled, all dreamed
Out into the white infinity
Worlds beyond are staring into the lonesome dark
The lonesome dark that is our world staring back
Once all level and sterile I noticed shadows as
endangered as ibex
I saw every forty-five degree angle and nothing
more
Pulled the flesh by hand, he said
He pulled the flesh by hand
I hear the clack, after I hear the tear
Oh, I loathe and fear
Once one is gone
That there will be no coming back

Case #43063

Joseph Robert Villari

Joseph Robert Villari is an advocate for all forms of the written word and actively writes and publishes in each. Possessing a deep curiosity for the world around him, he has earned a B.S. in Conservation Biology and is currently a graduate student at George Mason University, where he studies zoology. A native of the North American Mid Atlantic, he can often be found engaged in gritty, cross country road trips, hiking in forgotten lands with a 100-pound hound dog named Scout, or in a cool, dark room, preternaturally hunched over a keyboard.

CLAYTON HILL SANITARIUM

On the
Record

We are lucky to be sitting down with horror writer Ania Ahlborn. She is the creator of Seed, The Neighbours and her latest offering The Shuddering has hit Amazon last month. Thank you for spending a moment with us Ania.

Thanks for having me, Barry!

To kick things off, what was your first experience of the horror genre?

I have a reputation of my books reading like movies, and I guess I should chalk it up to my first horror exposure being on TV rather than on the page. I can't pinpoint an exact first—I was the type of kid who loved cheap TV horror and would watch it any chance I got. But my first truly terrifying experience was watching *The Exorcist* on New Year's Eve. I was something like nine or ten, my parents weren't home... it wasn't the best idea.

While you were growing up, did you have a favorite genre of horror that you would always gravitate to?

I was all over anything that was easily accessible, anything that was easy to sneak by the parents. Back in the 80's we had a lot of cheap horror running on certain networks, so I'd watch stuff like *Troll* and *Dolls*. Halloween is still my favorite time of year. We're doing the high-tech no-cable streaming-only TV thing at our house, but I still marathon classic 80's horror flicks throughout October. It's a weird form of childhood nostalgia.

You mention on your site that you grew up living next to a cemetery. Did that push you in the direction of horror, or do you think you would have found your way eventually?

I would have found my way regardless, but yes, we did live next to a cemetery—Forest Lawn, if I recall correctly. By the time I was sneaking through the hole in the fence and visiting tombstones, my head was already full of ghosts and goblins. That's probably why I visited the cemetery in the first place. Any normal kid would have kept their distance.

What age did you start writing in a serious nature and do you ever go back to old stories?

I started writing roughly around age ten, but I only started writing seriously after I graduated high school. That isn't to say that I didn't write during those eight or so years in between; I did, a *lot*. But it was all throwaway stuff. I never actually sat down and planned out characters or thought about plot. As for going back to old stories, not really; after so many years of banging away at a keyboard, you learn and grow. You have to let the old stuff go to continue moving forward.

You grew up in Poland but now you live in Albuquerque. How does the horror scene differ from country to country?

I have absolutely no idea. I was really young when we left Poland, and I've only had one opportunity to go back to visit since, so I haven't had the chance to explore Poland in that sort of way. But I imagine the scene there is far better than the scene here. Poland is beautiful, but there's a very brooding darkness to it. Lots of blood in the soil; its fertile ground for some incredibly dark stuff.

It's well documented that rejection is part of the writing process. If you do get a rejection letter, how do you process it before moving on?

If you're a writer and haven't gotten an honest-to-goodness rejection letter, you should submit a few queries just to get into the club. I got my share, but they never really got to me. I saved them for a while, though I don't know why. Maybe I was going to wallpaper one of the rooms with them. But finally I just started tossing them in the trash. I took on a "their loss" attitude and kept pushing ahead. You need thick skin to be in this business. If a rejection seriously gets you down, imagine what a scathing one-star review will do to you if you *do* get published.

Do you have any pet peeves when it comes to reading other writers work?

Unrealistic dialogue is the hardest to overlook. It's jarring. It makes me shake my head and tisk like a super-judgey mother.

I was looking at your main site and there is a great treasure trove of information on your blog, not to mention your Facebook and twitter posts. How do you find the time to maintain them all?

Honestly, it looks like I'm maintaining all of that stuff, but it's a ruse. Crafty time management and scheduling posts make it look like I'm toiling away in social media land, but I'm really not. If I have enough time to sit around and do that stuff, I feel like I'm not working hard enough.

With regards to social media, do you feel it is important for a writer to keep in touch with their readers – or is too much contact a bad thing?

I think there's a happy medium. I'm a huge fan of connecting with my readers. I respond to emails and tweets and Facebook posts if it's appropriate. But yeah, there should be a bit of mystery behind the author. I give away way too much about myself in my books already.

The Shuddering has been released as an audio book, how did you find that process and did you have much input into the finished article?

I don't have any input as far as audio books go. Unless you're hiring the voice actor yourself (which I can only guess would be extremely expensive), I don't think many authors have a say in what happens when it comes to this aspect of publishing. But, if I ever do have a say, my vote is for Christopher Walken to re-voice my entire oeuvre.

Do you have a set routine that you stick to when working on a book?

First drafts are always seven days a week with a word count goal of 25,000 per week, give or take. I don't always hit that goal. It's kind of crazy and I may back off a bit on my next go-round because it gets exhausting, but that's what I've stuck to for the past few books.

Can you tell us a little about the next book you have planned?
The next book is called *The Bird Eater*, and it's a contemporary take on haunted houses and super-creepy kids. I'm really excited about it because it's the novel that's given me the most trouble thus far. From where it started to where it ended up, I see it as a bit of a miracle. Lots and lots and lots of rewrites on that one.

What was the best piece of advice you ever received about writing?

Probably that old saying of "show, don't tell." Then again, if you're looking for writing advice and haven't read Stephen King's *On Writing*, you're missing out. It's a masterpiece that speaks to writers on multiple levels.

Finally before we let you go. Do you have a piece of advice for our readers who are looking to improve their writing?

Allow the first draft to suck, don't edit while you're writing it, don't gab about what you're writing, and for God's sake, don't show anyone your rough drafts. We creative types are stupidly sensitive beings. The last thing you need is your best friend giving you advice on how to improve your plot or your mother saying, "That's nice, dear" with less than 100% enthusiasm. It will stifle your creativity and destroy your need to finish telling the story. Keep what you're doing to yourself until you're happy with what you've got, and keep writing until it's finished. Everyday. Even if it's only a paragraph.

Thank you very much for spending time with us Ania, we hope the next book is a hit and we look forward to seeing what you have in store for us.

Thanks for having me!

https://www.aniaahlborn.com/

Can you describe for us what your workspace is like?

On the whole my workspace is quite neat and tidy. I am not really one for making that many paper notes, so there is little clutter. I work on my MacBook Pro most of the time so i can literally write wherever I happen to be.

At home though I have a small table in the corner of the living room. I work at this when I can and keep a stack of books on the table by authors who have inspired me, I also keep my own novel on this pile to keep me motivated.

Do you have a go-to gadget / app or service that you cannot live without?

My MacBook Pro is the most essential gadget I have as this is where I keep all of my notes, do my research and write. I also have to say I am permanently attached to my iPad as this allows me to keep up with all of my social media while working. I have also recently quit smoking so my E-cigarette is always near by.

Apps wise I use Pages to write so that is the most important one for me. Also, I have a Cheezburger app on my iPad that allows me to check Failblog as often as I want. This is very entertaining but can lead to a lot of wasted time.

Do you have a set routine while you work?

No, not as such. My wife works shifts and I am a stay at home Dad, and author. This means a lot of my time is spent looking after my little boy, Freddy.

I just try to write as often as I can. This can be at any time of the day or night when I get a little peace and quiet. I have always found that the period from midnight to about 4am is my most productive though.

What is the best piece of advice you have ever received?

Get an editor. I initially released my debut novel 'Beneath' after it had been proof read by three people (none of whom were professionals), and though they did do a great job, there were still a lot of spelling and grammatical errors. People who read the book initially on its release picked up on this and it lowered the books rating. most were saying it was a great story, but these errors let it down.

It was then that I found my editor, Jackie, and since she edited the second edition there have been no complaints about it. So, it was the best advice I was given, get your work professionally edited.
I chose to ignore it and it could have damaged my reputation permanently had I not rectified the situation.

Do you have a final piece of advice for our readers?

Relax and slow down. That is the key piece of advice I can give. It is important to work to deadlines, but it is bad for your writing to kill yourself in the process. After I had finished my first novel, I was in such a rush to get it out there that I made a lot of mistakes.
Also, I put a lot of pressure on myself to get my second book, 'Dark County' out as soon after as I could. Though I managed it I was constantly stressed at the time.

It got to the point where if I wasn't writing I felt like I letting myself down.

So, I took a holiday, A whole month off writing. When I started again, i felt much more relaxed, and was enjoying working on my next novel 'The Wilds', which I am hoping to release around Halloween.

At the end of the day if you put all this pressure on yourself, and don't enjoy what you are doing either your work will suffer, or you'll go crazy.

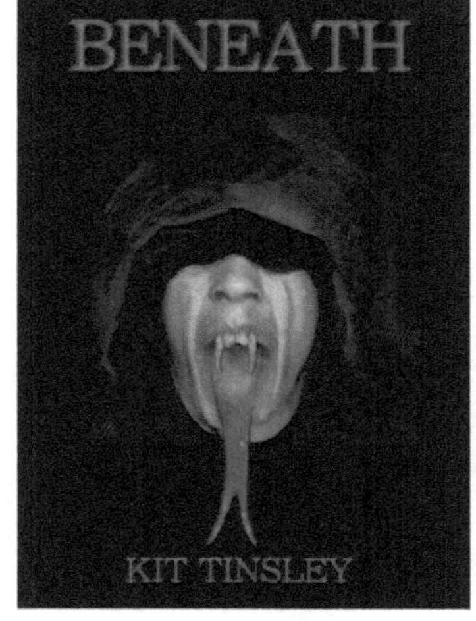

About Kit Tindley

Kit Tinsley was born in Shrewsbury, Shropshire, in 1978. When he was seven, he and his family moved to Lincolnshire. From an early age he started making up stories and characters. He has had a life ling love of horror in both books and film, it was these books by the like of Stephen King, James Herbert and Clive Barker, along with the films of Wes Craven, John Carpenter and Tobe Hooper that inspired him to create his own horror stories.

Kit studied English Literature and Media studies at DeMonfort University in Leicester, later teaching both subjects in secondary schools and colleges. During all of this time Kit was still coming up with stories and characters. After giving up teaching Kit got involved with independent film. He was commissioned to write a script for a low budget horror film in 2007, this was the start of his serious writing career. Though the script was drastically rewritten, and the film lost in post production hell Kit kept writing.

In 2011, while awaiting the birth of his son, Kit began work on his first novel 'Beneath', half way through

the book was put on hold due to the pressures of having a new baby in the house. Six month later Kit carried on with the book. It was completed late in 2012 and published in February 2013, to great early success, and reviews. Kit followed the book up with a collection of short stories, all set in Lincolnshire, called 'Dark County'.

Kit lives in Lincolnshire with his wife and son. The county he calls home is one of the biggest influences on his writing. It is a place of beauty and bleakness, of friendly people and isolation, and of light and dark. These are the things that permeate Kit's writing.

For More Info go to

http://www.kit-tinsley.com/

Hello horror lover.
If you've been suffering from a persistent desire for just a little more unpleasantness in your life, we have the answer:
NOCTURNAL TRANSMISSIONS
PODCAST
Nocturnal Transmissions is a fortnightly podcast featuring inspired performances of dark tales both old and new by voice artist Kristin Holland.
Find them at
nocturnaltransmissions.com.au
or wherever good podcasts are purveyed.

If you have any feedback or would like to leave a review please head over to Amazon and share your thoughts about Sanitarium.

Thank you for your time and we salute your
love for all things horror.

135